SCRAPPER JOHN

VALLEY OF THE SPOTTED HORSES

Other Avon Camelot Books by
Paul Bagdon
Featuring Scrapper John

SHOWDOWN AT BURNT ROCK
RENDEZVOUS AT SKULL MOUNTAIN

PAUL BAGDON is an ex-rodeo rider and horse trainer who has written a number of juvenile and western novels. He lives in Rochester, New York.

SCRAPPER JOHN
VALLEY OF THE SPOTTED HORSES

PAUL BAGDON

AN AVON CAMELOT BOOK

SCRAPPER JOHN: VALLEY OF THE SPOTTED HORSES is an original publica-
tion of Avon Books. This work has never before appeared in book form.

AVON BOOKS
A division of
The Hearst Corporation
1350 Avenue of the Americas
New York, New York 10019

Copyright a 1992 by Cloverdale Press
Published by arrangement with Cloverdale Press
Library of Congress Catalog Card Number: 91-93021
ISBN: 0-380-76416-4
RL: 6.4

First Avon Camelot Printing: March 1992

CAMELOT TRADEMARK REG. U.S. PAT. OFF. AND IN OTHER COUNTRIES. MARCA REGIS-
TRADA. HECHO EN U.S.A.

Printed in the U.S.A.

OPM 10 9 8 7 6 5 4 3 2

CHAPTER ONE

It was a crystal clear morning in the Montana Rockies, and the air was so pure it seemed like a boy could see all the way to Mexico. The sun had been up for barely an hour and was already starting to show its strength. Patches of morning fog were burning off the land and swirling into the blue sky.

Scrapper John Lewis and his father, Stone Pete, rode horseback through a valley of green pines, heading toward a snow-peaked mountain that towered over the valley. The night animals and birds had long since given up their hunting, and the creatures of the day were not yet about. Except for the gentle crunch of their horses' shod hooves on the thick carpet of pine needles, the silence was unbroken.

The light morning breeze toyed with Scrapper John's shoulder-length, blond hair, pushing it back from the dark skin of his forehead. His

1

fifteen-year-old body was lean, and the rifle-barrel straightness of his back made him look taller than he really was. The muscles under his loose-fitting deerskin shirt were hard from a lifetime of work on his father's trap lines.

Scrapper John's father, Stone Pete Lewis, was a huge man with rock hard muscles and brown eyes that always seemed to be laughing. Stone Pete's dark hair was also shoulder length. There were no barber shops in the Rocky Mountains—not much civilization of any kind for that matter. Both father and son wore snug-fitting denim pants and deerskin jackets, with fringes along their sleeves. Their moccasins were also made of dark deer hide and reached almost to their knees, like soft, laced boots.

There were no trails for Scrapper John and Stone Pete to follow. It was unlikely that the forest appeared on any map, and even if it did, animals, Indians, and mountain men were the only ones to pass through it. Running alongside Scrapper John's horse was his old friend, a wolf-dog named Musket.

Musket was the size of a timber wolf, and he looked like one, except that his fur was longer than a wolf's and the color of dusty brass. Musket's mother had been a Scottish collie owned by a sheepherder friend of Stone Pete, but his father had been a wandering Rocky Mountain wolf, and Musket had the teeth to prove it.

Scrapper John eased back on the reins of his pinto, Firearrow. A massive pine that seemed tall enough to touch the sky caught his attention.

High up the trunk, the bark had been broken and scratched away.

"Pa," he called. "Lookit this. Could a bear reach that high? If one did, I ain't about to argue with him if we meet up somewheres."

Stone Pete reined his chestnut stallion toward the tree. "It's a bear all right—ain't no doubt about that. Them gouges is deep, an' that tells me this bear has good claws that he wanted to sharpen up. He's gotta be the biggest danged grizzly I ever come across. He's reachin' up better'n ten feet on that pine."

Scrapper John shuddered for a quick moment. His father noticed it and smiled, his teeth startlingly white against the deep tan of his face. "Kinda scare you a tad, son?"

Scrapper John forced a smile. "No sir. I was jist thinkin' I might run down that bear an' eat him for breakfast."

Stone Pete roared with laughter, frightening a flock of birds that had been perched in a nearby tree. They turned their mounts back toward the snowy peak miles ahead.

Stone Pete had moved to the Rockies with his friend Sweetwater Eddy after the Civil War battle at Appomattox. As a sergeant, Stone Pete had seen more battles than he cared to remember in the bloody war between the states. He'd taken an oath that he'd never again fire a gun of any kind at a living creature for the rest of his life. He and Sweetwater Eddy had ridden to the Rockies to make their homes far from towns and cities. Even the lonely spot Stone Pete had found to

3

build his cabin wasn't far enough away for Sweetwater Eddy, who'd gone even farther into the mountains to live.

Stone Pete had built a log cabin and set out to win an Indian woman named Silent Fox from the Nez Perce tribe for his wife. It hadn't been easy. He'd been forced to fight five of Silent Fox's brothers hand to hand before asking her father for her hand in marriage.

Scrapper John remembered his mother well, although she had died of a fever when he was barely five years old. Scrapper John had her high cheekbones, and his skin glowed slightly amber under his year-round deep tan. His eyes, like those of his mother, were a deep, liquid brown. Where his blond hair came from no one knew. Stone Pete's was brown, and Silent Fox's had been ebony black.

Stone Pete's stallion snorted and tried to rear. The mountain man laughed, taking up slack in the reins and turning the horse tightly in a small circle. "This here horse is a bit feisty this mornin', ain't he Scrapper?"

"If he's more'n you can handle, step down, Pa. I'll learn him some manners." Scrapper John grinned.

Although Scrapper John was five-and-a-half feet tall and weighed only a hundred and twenty-five pounds, he was strong enough to lift two-thirds of that weight fairly easily. Living in the Rocky Mountains as the son of a mountain man had a way of turning a boy into a man in a hurry. Scrapper John was almost as fine a marksman with a bow and arrow as his father. He could throw his sheath knife at a knothole on a tree thirty feet away and strike it dead center nine times out of ten.

Stone Pete looked at his son, and his black eyes became serious for a moment. "Darned if you couldn't, boy. I got to say I never seen a hand with horses—with all animals—like yours. I swear you could learn a grizzly to play a guitar an' sing while he's strummin'."

"Maybe that ol' horse is mad cause you ain't given him a name yet. If I had gone an' traded six months' worth of prime pelts two days ago for a big red horse, I'd sure name him. How about calling him Snorty, Pa? He's always snortin' through his nose like he just done."

Stone Pete considered the name for a moment. He shook his head. "Nah. Snorty ain't right. A horse like this one needs a name he can be proud of. Somethin' as good as your Firearrow, there."

Some mischief glinted in Scrapper John's eyes. "Too bad he ain't a fast horse, Pa. If he was, you could name him Lightning or somethin' like that. But heck, he's too fat to git outta his own way. Poor ol' nag. Probably couldn't outrun a sick snail on the best day he ever had. Right, Pa?"

Stone Pete stood in his stirrups, peering ahead. They were passing out of the forest. A hundred yards or so ahead a sharp stone outcropping pointed to the sky like a finger. A field of buffalo grass, still glistening with dew, lay between the forest and the rise. On the other side of the wall of stone, he knew that a stream meandered through the field.

"You wouldn't be trying to set up some kinda horse race here, would you, Scrapper?" Stone Pete demanded. " 'Cause any man with a lick of sense could see that plow-puller you're settin' on ain't got the strength for no race."

"Talk don't win no races," Scrapper John answered, smiling at his father.

"No. It sure don't. But you got a lot to learn about runnin' horses. I need to tell you some things that can make all the difference in the world. For instance, boy, you don't know nothin' 'bout startin' a race."

Scrapper John sighed and relaxed in his saddle, looping the ends of his reins loosely around his saddle horn. "Okay, Pa," he said. "Tell me 'bout how to start a horse race."

"Well, there are two ways, boy. One is where one of the fellows counts down, an' you're off when he reaches 'go.' That one works good, but I kinda like the other one better."

"How's that one work?" Scrapper John asked.

"Like this!" Stone Pete bellowed, thumping his heels on the sides of his mount and leaning forward in his saddle. The huge stallion lunged ahead like a shot from a cannon, throwing clods of dirt and bits of grass from under his scrambling hooves.

Scrapper John recovered from his surprise in half a heartbeat, but his father was already several yards ahead of him. He fumbled his reins free of the saddle horn and banged his heels

6

against the pinto's sides. Firearrow threw himself after Stone Pete's horse, urged on by Scrapper John's whoops and yells.

The chestnut stallion was running hard, his body stretched in a full gallop. He thundered onto a narrow path that led across an open field covered with patches of emerald green buffalo grass. Firearrow hurled down the path, doing his level best to catch the larger horse ten yards ahead of him.

Scrapper John leaned ahead in the saddle, his face next to Firearrow's neck, his long blond hair pushed back from his tanned face by the speed of the pinto. At Scrapper John's right, Musket matched Firearrow's gallop, his pink tongue and white fangs showing in his open, wolflike muzzle.

Stone Pete tugged lightly on his reins. Just ahead, the outcrop of dark stone and dirt towered above the field. The stallion slowed the slightest bit, preparing for the turn at the wall. Stone Pete snapped a look back at Scrapper John.

"Git movin' or you lose, boy!" he yelled.

Scrapper John felt Firearrow gain slightly on his father's horse. "Go, Arrow! We're catchin' them!" he urged the pinto.

A strange scent struck Musket's nose, and the wolf-dog slowed his stride for the smallest part of a second. Suddenly, he broke into a volley of barks and snarls. Scrapper John glanced down at his dog just as Stone Pete's stallion blasted around the outcrop.

"I ain't got time to play, Musket," Scrapper John hollered. "I got to catch Pa!" Musket moved even closer to Firearrow, barking even more frantically, but Scrapper John was too busy to pay attention. The turn around the outcrop was rushing at him. He wanted to take it as fast as Firearrow could manage without tangling his legs and going down.

Musket saw that Scrapper John was ignoring him. Crazy with the heavy smell that had been carried to him by the breeze, he launched himself at his master and Firearrow. Startled, the mountain boy hauled back on the reins. Firearrow stumbled, scrambled, and caught his balance just as he began the turn.

When Stone Pete's new stallion slammed around the curve, a laugh of victory died in the mountain man's throat. A massive, humpbacked grizzly blocked his path. The giant bear, its left eye socket empty and sharply pink against its dirty black fur, snarled a challenge at the horse and the man that had suddenly burst into view.

The horse veered and stumbled, its eyes wide with fear. Stone Pete's right hand went for the bowie knife in the sheath on his belt. The bear struck first, its three-inch-long claws dragging deep bloody furrows along the horse's side, tearing through flesh and muscle. The chestnut stallion hit the ground hard on its side, whinnying in pain and terror. Stone Pete slammed to the ground, too, diving to one side. The shiny twelve-inch blade of his bowie knife glinted with sunlight.

The grizzly roared, its one small black eye bloodshot and flashing with fury. Its fangs were yellow with age but as sharp as razors. He lumbered toward the chestnut stallion. The horse, badly wounded and covered with blood, tried to get up.

Stone Pete's roar of anger was as loud as the grizzly's. Two long strides put the mountain man in front of the injured horse. "Get back, dang you!" Stone Pete hollered at the bear. "You done enough to this horse—now you got to come past me!"

Just then, Scrapper John galloped around the outcrop and saw what was happening. Stone Pete, his bowie knife held out in front of him, turned his head to yell to his son. The bear struck at the same time, moving faster than seemed possible for such a huge animal. One giant paw slammed against the hand holding the bowie knife. The grizzly's other paw grabbed Stone Pete in a deadly hug.

Firearrow skidded to a stop and reared in panic. Scrapper John dove from his saddle. He hit the ground, rolled across his back and shoulders with his head safely tucked, and was on his feet and running toward the grizzly in less than a second. He grabbed up a short length of a branch from the ground as he ran, clutching it like a bat.

Musket ran past him, snarling. The wolf-dog threw himself at the grizzly, sinking his teeth deep into the bear's leg. Stone Pete was held tightly against the bear's chest by a huge, furry foreleg. His eyes were closed, and he wasn't moving. Scrapper John swung the branch with all the power he had, hitting the bear again and again.

Musket released his hold on the bear's leg and dropped back. His instinct told him to fight as a wolf fights, to strike again and again doing as much damage as possible in the shortest time. He hurled himself at the enemy again. Scrapper John used the stout branch to pound at the bear's forelegs and the giant paws that were crushing the life out of Stone Pete.

The bear swung its gigantic head from side to side, the empty eye socket inches from Scrapper John's face. The grizzly's breath was hot and wet, and stank of rotten meat and fresh blood.

Scrapper John slammed the bear again. His face ran with sweat, and his breath rasped in his throat. Musket's fangs snapped at the grizzly's legs. The grizzly hooked its claws into Stone Pete's back and flung him away. Then it dropped from its two hind legs to all fours. It backed away from its attackers, still swinging one deadly paw at the boy and wolf-dog.

Scrapper John stepped back, his thick branch ready in front of him. "Musket—let him go!" he yelled. Musket opened his mouth and let go of the grizzly's fur, quickly backing away from the terrible beast.

The grizzly roared angrily from deep in its throat and glared into Scrapper John's eyes. Then it backed away a few feet, swung around, and plodded off into the brush.

Scrapper John stood tensely, breathing hard. Musket waited beside the mountain boy, panting hard with his long tongue shiny and wet between his razor sharp teeth. The silence after the battle seemed louder than the fight itself. Scrapper John forced himself to wait another half minute to make sure the bear wasn't going to charge again, clutching his branch tightly just in case.

After a moment, he dropped his weapon and raced to Stone Pete's still body, which lay where it had been thrown by the ferocious grizzly.

CHAPTER TWO

Stone Pete's eyes were open, but his face was a sickly white color, despite his deep tan. He breathed hard, as if he wasn't getting enough air. The front of his deerskin jacket was soaked with blood.

"Pa!" Scrapper John said frantically. "Pa . . ."

His father forced a smile to his face, but it wasn't very convincing. When he spoke, his voice was barely a loud whisper. "You done good, Scrap. You an' Musket run that grizzly off jist as neat as can be. I seen most of it. I'm right proud of you."

Scrapper John's hands trembled as he crouched next to his father, pushing the long strands of dark hair away from the man's face.

"How bad's my horse?" Stone Pete rasped.

Scrapper John looked quickly around the area. Both mounts were gone.

"He must have run off, Pa. Firearrow's gone, too."

For a moment, Stone Pete's smile was real. "Run off? That horse ain't never gonna run nowhere again." He coughed, and his face twisted in pain. "He was hurt bad, John. He ain't gonna make it. He went off to die, is what he done." Stone Pete coughed again and went on. "Never even got to name him. Nice horse. Sure could cover ground in a hurry, couldn't he?"

"You'll have a whole herd of even better horses, Pa," Scrapper John said quietly. "Soon's you heal up."

Stone Pete began to say something but stopped. He closed his eyes. "Git me some water, John," he whispered.

Scrapper John dashed to the stream and tugged a large, frayed bandanna from his pants pocket. He soaked the cloth in the water and hurried back to his father. Stone Pete sucked the wetness from the cloth.

While Stone Pete was drinking, Firearrow, winded and breathing fast and hard, walked slowly from the forest into the clearing and over to Scrapper John. The pinto's sides and chest were soaked with sweat and white froth, and the reins trailed on the ground on either side, but he didn't appear to have been injured.

"Looks like it's up to you, John," said Stone Pete. His voice sounded stronger after drinking. "We're out here a good five miles from home, an' I sure can't walk to the cabin. What're you gonna do?"

Scrapper John struggled to keep his voice even. "Jist what you done that time we was walkin'

13

the trap lines an' I sprained my leg so bad. I'm gonna rig up a travois an' haul you home."

Stone Pete smiled a little. "Good thinkin'. You go an' do that. I'm gonna shut my eyes for a bit."

Scrapper John stood beside his father for a moment, watching the uneven rising and falling of the man's chest. Musket poked his long muzzle into the mountain boy's hand and whined softly.

"We'll get you home, Pa," the boy said. Stone Pete stirred slightly but didn't speak.

Scrapper John found his father's knife on the ground where it had landed after the bear knocked it from his hand. He loped a hundred yards to where the forest began, with Musket running out in front, sniffing the air for any scent of the bear. Scrapper John used the bowie knife to cut down a pair of twelve-foot-high saplings and trim the branches from them. The blade cut through the wood easily. To kill a young tree went against what Scrapper John had been taught, but he had no choice. He quickly gathered up what he'd cut down and carried it back to where his father lay.

Scrapper John set the two long, thin sapling trunks side by side, in a V-shape about three feet apart at one end and a foot apart at the other. Then he took the trimmed branches and lay them across the two saplings. Some of the vines he'd wrenched free at the edge of the woods had thorns and brambles, and his palms were soon bleeding. He didn't notice the pain. Using the vines as cord, he tied the branches between the two thin tree trunks.

Scrapper John worked quickly and quietly. The travois wasn't as straight or as neat as the one Stone Pete had built years earlier, but Scrapper John was satisfied with it. It would do the job, and that's all that counted. Stone Pete groaned when his son eased him onto the branches between the poles.

Scrapper John put the ends of the two long saplings through the stirrups on Firearrow's saddle and secured them with rope from his saddlebag. The boy grabbed the saddle horn with both hands and swung himself into the saddle without using the stirrups. He kept a tight grip on the reins. Firearrow was still spooked by the grizzly and had become skittish.

It wasn't going to be an easy trip, but Scrapper John didn't have a choice. He couldn't carry his father. The travois was the only solution. He eased Firearrow ahead. Stone Pete groaned as the travois began moving, but didn't awaken.

Scrapper John kept his horse at a very slow walk. Musket ran ahead of the pinto, zigzagging back and forth and every so often swinging back to do the same in the rear. Scrapper John couldn't help but marvel at Musket, who was faithfully guarding against the return of the grizzly bear.

They reached the log cabin a couple of hours later, although to Scrapper John the journey seemed to take forever. Built on a small rise halfway up the side of a mountain, it was fancy by the standards of mountain men. But Stone Pete had known he'd be bringing a wife to the cabin, and he had wanted it to be special for her.

The cabin was made from logs Stone Pete had cut and cured, and roofed with slabs of slate he'd gathered in the foothills and hauled back on horseback. There was real glass in the windows—which was usually unheard of in the homes of mountain men. The cabin was long and narrow, and a covered porch ran along the front. The bedrooms were at one end, while the living space and kitchen were at the other. A stream ran past the back of the cabin, so fresh, cold water was always close by.

The cabin faced west. Stone Pete always loved sitting on the porch with his wife and baby, and later just with his son, watching the sun set behind the snow-covered peak of a majestic unnamed mountain that rose in the distance.

Scrapper John stopped Firearrow at the front door of the cabin and swung off the pinto's back. On the travois, Stone Pete was breathing with short, fast breaths, and his face was soaked with sweat. The boy placed his hands under his father's arms. As gently as possible he dragged him into the cabin. There were several tanned, furry hides on the floor in front of the huge stone fireplace. Scrapper John eased his father onto one of the skins and covered him with another. Stone Pete's eyes opened. He looked very pale and very tired.

"We home, Scrapper?" he asked.

"We sure are, Pa," the mountain boy said, kneeling to speak to his father. "I'll fetch some

16

water an' clean you up some an' then get a fire goin'. I'll cook up some stew an' soup, an' you'll feel a heap better. . . ."

Stone Pete reached over and took his son's hand in his own. "I ain't got much time, son. Soup ain't gonna do me no good. You seen what that grizzly done to me. You heard me coughin' like a ol' moose."

"But Pa . . ."

"Hush, now. Ain't nobody lives forever, not you an' not me. I ain't 'fraid of nothin' 'cept leavin' you all alone." Stone Pete smiled. "An' you're pretty much growed up, anyway. I'm right proud of you, son."

Scrapper John felt totally helpless. The raspiness of his father's voice frightened him as much as what the man said.

Stone Pete's eyes closed. Scrapper John pressed his ear to his father's chest and listened, holding his breath. The heartbeat fluttered like a bird caught in the house. He straightened up and stood next to his father, his mind racing.

Stone Pete had always handled any doctoring that needed to be done. Scrapper John had learned how to brew tea from the skins of apples for treating an upset stomach, and he knew how to rig a sling. He even knew how to use the big sewing needle and black fishing line to make a couple of stitches to close a cut. But Scrapper John knew his father was far beyond the help that apple skins or fishing line stitches could offer.

The mountain boy looked out the window. Evening was coming. In the distance he could see snow on the mountain peaks, even though it was still summer. There was one man who could help—Sweetwater Eddy, his father's old friend and their nearest neighbor. He lived over ten miles away. The trip would take three hours each way if he pushed Firearrow hard across the difficult terrain. Scrapper John hated to leave his father alone, but he had no choice.

He whistled softly out the open window for Musket. In seconds the wolf-dog stood next to him.

"Stay here, Musket," he said. "Watch Pa real close." Then Scrapper John turned and hurried from the cabin.

The mountain boy looked his horse over closely, checking the set of the pinto's iron shoes. He let the horse drink at the stream behind the cabin, then mounted up. Although Firearrow was still skittish from the bear attack much earlier in the day, Scrapper John was able to use the pinto's nervousness to his own advantage. He let Firearrow run off his excess energy by holding him to a quick pace.

Sweetwater Eddy lived in a small cabin in the sharp "V" of a valley beyond a tower of stone called Fremont Peak. Scrapper John and his father had visited him only eight or ten times over the years. To get there, Scrapper John had to find his way across some of the roughest country in the Rockies.

Sweetwater Eddy had earned his nickname

during the Great War Between the States, when he was a rifleman in the platoon led by Stone Pete Lewis. No matter where the fighting was, Eddy could always be counted on to find a pool or spring where the water was cold and clean. The men joked that given half a chance, Eddy could probably find cold water on the sun. And Stone Pete had often told Scrapper John that during the war, Sweetwater Eddy's medical skills had saved many men's lives.

Darkness fell as Scrapper John urged his pinto quickly through the forest. Some mountain peaks etched sharply against the star-filled sky told him he was heading in the right direction. Rocks and stones littered the terrain. It was dangerous to ride too fast. A horse could easily step on a rock he hadn't seen, twist a leg, and go down hard, possibly snapping the bone.

Coyotes wailed in the forest all around Scrapper John, some very close to him and his horse. He'd never heard so many of them together before, and their howls sent chills up and down his spine. Eventually he spied the towerlike outcropping of Fremont's Peak. As he topped a rise, Sweetwater Eddy's cabin came into view, a dark shape in a spot of moonlight on one side of a small valley.

Scrapper John raced to the cabin, threw himself off Firearrow, and pounded on the door with his fists. Suddenly, a loud, sharp crack split the air. The wooden door exploded, with splinters flying into his face!

A man roared from the darkness behind Scrapper John. "Bring them paws up real slow-like, an' say your name loud an' clear," the deep voice said, "or I'll shoot you dead!"

CHAPTER THREE

Scrapper John spun around and raised his hands above his head. He stood perfectly still, hardly daring to breathe. His throat felt as dry as desert sand.

"I coulda put that one right 'tween your eyes if I wanted," the man's voice thundered from the darkness. "Now, say your name, an' tell me what you're doin' here, an' I might let you live!"

"Scrap . . . Scrapper John Lewis."

Moccasins thumped and scratched on the dirt, and Sweetwater Eddy stood in front of him, a Sharps buffalo rifle held in his right hand. He had the huge thick arms of a blacksmith and the smoldering eyes of a timber wolf. His long hair and thick beard were matted and shaggy. In the starlight they seemed to glow like a furry halo around the mountain man's craggy face.

"John? Scrapper John? What in tarnation are you doin' up here in the middle of the night? I coulda plugged you an' asked questions later! Don't Stone Pete know better'n to let his cub wander off?"

Scrapper John grabbed Sweetwater Eddy's shoulders, but when he tried to speak only a few hoarse sounds emerged from his throat. Eddy shoved the door open and pushed Scrapper John inside. He handed the boy a tin can filled with cool water. Scrapper John gulped the liquid down. Then he began to talk, his words spilling over each other.

"Wait now!" Eddy hollered. "Calm down a tad an' start all over again. What's this about your pa an' a bear?"

Scrapper John started his story again, forcing himself to speak slowly. As he spoke, Sweetwater Eddy scraped a sulphur match on the wall and touched the flame to the wick of an oil lantern. A dim, warm light filled the interior of the small log cabin. While Scrapper John was still talking, the mountain man began pulling things off shelves and dropping them into a deer-hide sack.

"No wonder your pa hung that 'Scrapper' name on you. You're as much of a fighter as he is," Sweetwater Eddy said, giving John a strange look. Then he asked, "Did your pa say where he was hurtin' worst?"

"No sir. He was passed out most of the time an' talkin' funny when he wasn't. He said my ma's name a couple times, an' he hardly never talks about her."

Sweetwater Eddy nodded. "Yeah. I know. How'd his breathin' sound?"

"Not good. Seemed like he couldn't pull in enough air, an' there was kind of a rattling noise when he breathed out."

Eddy grabbed a glass jar full of gray powder from a shelf and dropped it in the sack. "Was he bleedin' bad?"

"No, sir. He was cut up some, an' his back was bleedin', but there wasn't no blood pouring from him anywhere. His face felt hot, an' he was sweatin' a lot when I left."

"He's alone, then?"

" 'Cept for my dog, Musket. He'll watch Pa real close." A terrible thought struck the boy. "Did I do wrong? Should I have stayed with Pa?"

Sweetwater Eddy put his hand on Scrapper John's shoulder and squeezed hard. "No, you was exactly right. Wasn't nothin' you coulda done for Pete 'cept get some help." His eyes burned into Scrapper John's, and he kept his hold on the boy's shoulder. "I got to tell you this, John. It don't sound good. That grizzly had ahold of your Pa for too long. Them bears is twice as strong as a man. Some of Pete's ribs coulda been busted, an' the sharp edges coulda cut into his lungs. If that's what happened, I can't save him. You got to know that an' be ready for whatever happens."

For the first time since the battle with the old grizzly, tears gathered in Scrapper John's eyes and ran down his cheeks. He tried to turn away from Sweetwater Eddy, but the mountain man wouldn't let him go.

"Ain't no shame in cryin' for a man like Stone Pete Lewis," he said gently. "No shame at all. The Shoshone Indians believe that tears shed 'bout a man go to water his own special garden in the next world."

Sweetwater Eddy let go of the boy's shoulder and reached into a square tin can resting on a shelf above the fireplace. He dropped six bullets for his buffalo rifle into his shirt pocket. "That bear could still be around your place," he said. "I got to admire Stone Pete for keepin' his word 'bout never carryin' nor usin' a gun, but that don't mean I agree with him. If he had a Winchester with him, or even a pistol, when he met up with that one-eyed outlaw bear, he wouldn't be in the fix he's in right now."

"Eddy—I don't mean no disrespect, but we're burnin' time standin' here jawin'. Let's get . . ."

"You keep your drawers on, boy," Sweetwater Eddy snapped. He looked around the small cabin slowly and then peered into the sack. "I reckon I got everything." He held the lantern to his face and blew out the flame. "Let's make tracks, then. Like you said, we're burnin' time standin' here jawin'."

Sweetwater Eddy slung the leather sack over his shoulder and stepped out of the cabin. Scrapper John followed. The coyotes immediately started yelping and yipping in the forest around the cabin. The boy looked around curiously, trying to catch sight of the animals. He'd never heard so many in one place before.

"Shaddup, you buncha knuckleheads!" Eddy

24

hollered at the darkness. "It's jist me an' a friend!"

"You've trained coyotes?" Scrapper John asked.

"Nah." Eddie grunted. "Critters like them can't be trained. I feed this bunch a lot, an' they hang around here. Good guards is what they are, but they ain't pets. A man could probably teach a snake to fly 'fore he could train a coyote."

"Why don't you get yourself a dog? Dogs are good guards, too."

Sweetwater Eddy's face went hard and grim. He turned away and spoke without looking at Scrapper John. "Dogs is friends. I don't need no friends. Me an' your Pa joined up with the Union Army 'long with almost a hundred other fellers. They was friends of mine. Only Pete an' a couple other come outta the war. No sir, one thing I don't need is friends. They got a bad habit of disappearing."

The mountain man caught himself rambling on and turned back to Scrapper John. "My horse is out back. I'll saddle him an' meet you here. You drink some more water an' tend whatever needs tendin' to, cause I ain't pullin' rein to let you find a tree to water, hear me, Scrapper John?"

The mountain man soon returned, leading a tall black stallion. The man and boy mounted their horses.

"Follow me, but don't step on my heels," Sweetwater Eddy told John. "If I git too far ahead, whistle out, an' I'll slow down till you catch up. We'll keep on movin' at a good rate, but it won't do Stone Pete nor anyone else no good if we kill our horses. Your pinto already done a hard ten miles, so don't bust him down. He'll git you there without you pushin' him too hard. We'll stop 'bout halfway an' let the horses drink an' rest for ten minutes or so."

"We don't need to rest," Scrapper John urged. "I say we let the horses drink an' then keep . . ."

"Don't sass me, boy. I'm in charge here."

"I ain't sassin' you, Eddy. But my pa needs you real bad."

"Maybe. But a dead horse ain't gonna git me to him. We do it my way." Eddy's voice softened. "You love ol' Stone Pete more'n anyone or anything, don't you, boy?"

"Yes, sir. I sure do."

Sweetwater Eddy nodded. His voice turned gruff again. "Well, let's move out."

Sweetwater Eddy rode his tall black stallion as comfortably and naturally as Scrapper John rode Firearrow. But Eddy's way of covering ground was different. He rarely urged his mount beyond a lope but kept him moving at a fast, flowing jog that ate up distance surprisingly fast. Scrapper John matched Firearrow's pace to the black stallion's, lagging ten feet behind but sticking to Sweetwater Eddy's back like a shadow.

When they stopped at a shallow pool, Firearrow was wet with sweat, but Eddie's mount was breathing easily and barely damp. Scrapper John was impressed by Sweetwater Eddy's style of distance riding.

The boy splashed water over his face and chest

after drinking. "Where'd you learn to travel like that?" he asked.

Eddy looked surprised. "From your people, boy. From a Nez Perce warrior. Horses go down or git lame if a man don't know how to use 'em, an' that means a Nez Perce's scalp could end up decoratin' a Blackfoot tepee. See, they set a pace and keep to it. They don't try to burn up the ground—they jist keep on movin' steady an' sure. That's all there is to it."

The boy nodded. He turned Eddy's words, "your people" over in his mind. He'd always realized that he was half Indian and half white, but he thought of himself as part of each, not belonging to one or the other. He wondered if someday he'd have to make a choice between the two groups and what that decision would be.

"You 'bout ready, son?"

Sweetwater Eddy was in his saddle, looking down at the boy.

Scrapper John drew a pair of long, deep breaths and mounted Firearrow. "Ready," he said.

The moon rose, and its light made the ground almost silvery white. Bushes, trees, and rocks stood out clearly. When they arrived at Stone Pete and Scrapper John's cabin, it looked dark and lonely. Musket's throaty growl reached them when they were still a hundred yards away.

"Let him know it's you, John," Eddy said.

"Musket—hush, boy!"

The snarling stopped immediately. Scrapper John jumped off his horse and dashed ahead of the mountain man. He burst into the cabin and dropped to the floor at his father's side. Stone Pete's forehead was damp and very hot. He opened his eyes. "Scrap?" he asked in a whisper.

"I brought Sweetwater Eddy, Pa. He's . . ."

"I'm right here, Pete," Eddy said, kneeling next to his old friend. "I'm gonna take a look-see to find out if that bear done you any damage." He turned to Scrapper John. "Fetch a lantern, an' bring somethin' damp to wipe his face."

Scrapper John set the oil lantern on the floor and struck a match to it. As Sweetwater Eddy pulled back the tanned hide blanket covering Stone Pete, the boy hurried off to wet some cloths. He returned in less than a minute, but the blanket was already back over his father. Eddy crouched to one side, holding Stone Pete's hand in his own.

"He wants to talk to you, John," Sweetwater Eddy said. "Set close to him. His voice is fadin'."

Scrapper John knelt beside his father and leaned over him. Stone Pete's eyes blazed with fever. His voice trembled. It was barely a whisper.

"Ain't no use tryin' to convince you I'm gonna make it, son. I ain't. But . . ."

"You'll be fine, Pa! Eddy will fix you up good as new," Scrapper John said rapidly. "Why, you'll . . ."

"Listen to your Pa, John," Sweetwater Eddy interrupted gently. "He's right. There's nothin' I can do. Nothin' nobody can do. I'll leave you alone for a spell." Sweetwater Eddy clutched Stone Pete's hand for a long moment. Their eyes met and locked together. Neither man spoke. Then Eddy turned and left the cabin.

"You listen up, Scrapper," Stone Pete whispered. "I want you to go to your ma's people. Dark Eagle Walking is your grandpa. You tell him I'm gone after . . . after all this. Spend some time there with him. Keep away from our cabin for a while."

Stone Pete coughed, and pain seemed to flood across his face. It was a long time before he spoke again. Outside, the moon was bright, and its white light flooded through the cabin window.

"All you got to do is what's right, son," Stone Pete continued finally. "Make sure you laugh every day, an' don't never quit when you're dead sure you're in the right. Hear me?"

"Yes, sir," Scrapper John forced himself to say, despite the choking pain in his throat.

"Not much else I can tell you. If I done right raisin' you, you'll have as good a life as I did." Stone Pete struggled to a half-sitting position and pulled his son close. Outside, a mass of dark clouds blocked the moon. Musket pointed his wolflike muzzle at the sky and howled, his long wail splitting the darkness. The eerie sound echoed across the hills and faded like a memory. Holding John tightly, Stone Pete breathed his last breath.

When the first red light of dawn appeared in the east, Sweetwater Eddy and Scrapper John went to work. Neither said a word. The soil was dry on top but rich and dark after the first few shovelfuls. The only sound was their spades striking bits of stone and rock as they dug. Musket lay on one side of the grave, his muzzle resting on his forepaws. His eyes didn't leave Scrapper John, and every so often he whined deep in his throat.

Sweetwater Eddy looked down at the cabin from the small rise where they were digging. "Pretty spot," he said. "From here, Pete can see all 'round. Them mountain peaks off to the east was always favorites of his."

Scrapper John stopped working and straightened up, clutching his shovel. His eyes wandered to where Firearrow stood in the paddock down by the cabin.

Sweetwater Eddy noticed the boy's gaze. "Why don't you go down to your horse for a spell? I'll finish up here. Sometimes, bein' with an animal is better'n bein' with a human when you've had a loss like yours. A horse won't say nothin' stupid like most folks will—includin' me. You go on, John. Ain't much more here to do, an' I'll do it. Almost deep enough now."

Scrapper John nodded his thanks to Eddy and dropped his shovel. He walked to the paddock slowly. Long ago, his father had told him about an Indian tradition, and he turned it over and over in his mind. Firearrow nickered at him when he approached and pushed his velvety muzzle against the boy's neck. He opened the gate and entered the small fenced area. The pinto had a rawhide field halter over his head. He watched the boy expectantly, waiting for a treat or to be saddled. Scrapper John ran his eyes over the animal's sleek, tightly muscled body, proud of the condition his horse was in. Then the mountain boy spoke quietly.

"Firearrow, I know that lots of Indian tribes honor their dead by letting one of their finest horses go free. That way the spirit of the horse will be free to join the warrior who died. The Nez Perce do it, an' so do the Arapahos an' the Blackfeet."

Scrapper John moved the halter forward, easing it gently over the horse's delicate ears and sliding it off his muzzle.

"You been a real good horse, Firearrow." A small smile appeared on John's face. "Maybe you might even have caught up with that stallion of Pa's yesterday." The grin got larger. "But I kinda doubt it. That big ol' boy could fly. You was doin' right good, though. 'Member Pa bet you an' me couldn't make it to Sandy Ridge an' back 'fore nightfall that time? An' how we did anyway, so I spread lots of that red sand under Pa's sleepin' skins that night when we got back without sayin' nothin' to him."

Scrapper John placed the field halter over a fence post and went around the pinto, picking up one hoof at a time. He used the back edge of his sheath knife to pry loose the metal shoes and checked each hoof to make sure the nails were free. He used his fingers to tug the nails from the tops of each hoof.

" 'Member the first time I put shoes on you? I was scared I was gonna lame you up for good. But I didn't. Pa was a good teacher. Sure was

31

scary drivin' them first few nails. Pa stood there grinnin' like a mountain cat, sayin', 'Jist do it, boy. Winter's gonna set in 'fore you git steel under that tangle-footed ol' nag.' "

Scrapper John held the four horseshoes in one hand and stroked Firearrow with the other. His voice cracked when he said quietly, "You go an' be free, Firearrow. You'll find one of them bands of wild horses quick enough. An' one day, you go to Stone Pete Lewis. He'll be waitin' for you. You ain't gonna be lonely."

He slapped the pinto sharply on the rump. Firearrow eyed the boy, surprised and a little confused. Scrapper John slapped the horse's rump again. The pinto snuffed loudly through his nose and spun away from the boy.

"Go!" Scrapper John shouted, flapping his arms. The pinto started off at a jog. "Go, Firearrow!" John shouted again. This time the horse broke into a gallop. In a few moments even the sound of hoofbeats was gone. Scrapper John began walking back to the grave site. His steps were a little stronger than they had been earlier, and he held his head a bit higher.

Scrapper John and Sweetwater Eddy patted down the last few shovelfuls of earth on Stone Pete's grave with the backs of their spades. When they were finished they stood quietly for a long time.

"What're you goin' to do now, John?"

"I ain't sure, Eddy. Maybe I'll jist see what happens. Maybe going to see my grandfather with the Nez Perce like my pa told me to is a good idea. I'll be back in time to run Pa's winter trap lines, no matter what."

Sweetwater Eddy cleared his throat and looked off at the distant, snow-capped peaks. "I reckon I'm all through here. I'd best git back. I got me a coyote ma what had a hard time birthin' her kits. I been feedin' the little ones for her 'cause she's awful weak."

"Thanks for comin', Eddy."

"No call to thank me." Sweetwater Eddy cleared his throat again. Under his thick, matted beard it looked like the mountain man was blushing. "Thing is, John, what I said before ain't true. 'Bout friends, I mean. I . . . see . . . me an' you, we're friends, ain't we? Jist like I was friends with Stone Pete?"

A huge smile flooded across the boy's face. He put his hand out to shake with Eddy, but the mountain man moved past it and pulled Scrapper John into a big, strong hug.

CHAPTER FOUR

After Sweetwater Eddy rode off, it didn't take Scrapper John long to put his gear together. He gathered up a few days' supply of jerked venison and placed it in a softly tanned sack, along with a fifty-foot coil of Manila rope. He added a block of sulphur matches that had been dipped in wax to make them waterproof. He found a length of fish line with a hook and a lump of lye soap and dropped them into the sack. He found his whetstone, which he'd need to keep his arrows and his knife sharp. Then he slung his quiver, loaded with fifteen broadheaded arrows, over his shoulder. He picked up his bow and walked out into the sunlight.

There was no lock on the door. He pulled it shut behind him. Musket stood next to Scrapper John, looking up into the boy's face. His tail moved back and forth slowly, and he whined. The sounds were almost like human speech. Musket had done it since he was a puppy, and Scrapper John and his father had gotten used to the strange sounds. He reached down and scratched behind Musket's ears.

"Ready, partner?" he asked. "You better be. 'Cause we're goin' on a trip, an' what we come across is anybody's guess." The mountain boy and his wolf-dog started walking due west, directly in line with the arc of the setting sun.

The first night out, Scrapper John and Musket made camp beside a fast-moving stream that wandered through the foothills. Like most mountain men and all Indians, Scrapper John didn't measure distance in miles. In the Rockies, a place only five miles away could take several days to reach because of canyons, high peaks, and rivers or streams swollen by rain. He was satisfied with his progress, and he was bone tired from the events of the day and night before.

Scrapper John dug a half dozen fat worms out of the soil and in a matter of minutes caught three good-sized trout. He cleaned the fish effortlessly, his hands moving quickly and surely. Musket wolfed down the entrails from the trout. Scrapper John tossed the backbones from the fish into the stream to be carried off and out of Musket's reach. Bones like that could lodge in a dog's throat and cause the animal to choke.

Scrapper John slid the slabs of firm white trout onto a thick green stick and roasted them over a small camp fire. He washed his meal down with stream water. Then he gathered armfuls of soft grass for his bed. He unfolded a six-by-four-foot piece of oilcloth from his sack and put it over the grass. Musket stretched out next to Scrapper John, and together they listened to the night noises before the boy dropped off to a deep sleep.

While Scrapper John slept, Musket rose from his place several times to sniff the air. Once, he growled quietly but lost the scent that had teased him and curled up again. Far off thunder roared dully. Patches of clouds, dark and heavy with rain, drifted across the moon. The wolf-dog was on his feet again, pacing nervously, his muzzle pointed straight up, sniffing the air once more. He caught nothing but the scent of the distant storm in the breeze. Musket lay down and closed his eyes.

Daylight and the sound of rushing water tugged Scrapper John from his sleep. He sat up and rubbed his eyes in surprise. The stream had changed from a sparkling clear brook barely three feet across to a mud- and silt-choked river, sweeping small bushes and logs along in its racing torrents. Scrapper John got up and quickly folded his oilcloth.

"Lots of rain upstream last night," he said to Musket. The dog answered his master with high-pitched whines that brought a smile to the mountain boy's face. "Good thing it didn't rain down here, or we'd be soaking wet."

Quail were plentiful in the area, and John could easily have brought one down with an arrow. Instead, he gnawed on a few pieces of jerky. He washed quickly, scooping handfuls of the gritty water up to his face. Musket caught a thick knot of jerky Scrapper John tossed to him but didn't ask for more. The boy watched his dog curiously. Jerky was Musket's favorite treat, and he'd never before been satisfied with only a single piece of it.

"What's up, boy?" he asked. The hairs along Musket's spine rose, and he trotted in small worried circles around his master. Scrapper John looked slowly around him, his trained eyes probing for any sign of something out of order. For a moment he felt as if he were being watched. When he saw nothing, he laughed at himself for letting Musket make him feel edgy.

He waved at Musket. "Go on out there an' nose around, partner. Ain't nothin' to be afraid of. You're as edgy as an ol' bull moose this mornin'."

It was a fine morning for walking. Scrapper John followed the stream, in no hurry to cover ground. He used his bowie knife to chop a straight branch off a tree that had been uprooted by the torrent and flung on the shore. He strode along, poking his new walking stick out in front of him at each step.

A dead tree being whisked along on the swift currents of the stream caught Scrapper John's eye. He saw something move on it and looked more closely. A nest of rattlesnakes turned and twisted on the log, their pointed heads darting about, their forked tongues red, their fangs snow white. Their rattles, looking like a string of buttons, whirred crazily. There were at least a dozen of them, maybe twice that. It was impossible to count, because they were entwined together, writing and striking at one another. Their home in the dead log had been cut loose by the driving rain. Now, the log was a raft of death.

Soon it was noon, and the sun was high and hot. Scrapper John sat under a tree to eat his lunch. He eased his quiver and sack to the ground and leaned his bow against the tree. He smiled as he chewed on tough, salty jerky. When he was hungry enough, he realized, even jerky tasted good. Musket was still acting nervous. The mountain boy watched his dog, trying to figure out what was troubling him.

For the second time that day, Scrapper John had a strange feeling that he and Musket weren't alone. This time he stood, grabbing his bow. He notched an arrow and crouched next to a tree, his eyes sweeping the woods around him. He'd just about decided that nothing was wrong when Musket burst into a volley of almost frenzied barking and ran into the woods.

Scrapper John set off at a run, his bow and notched arrow grasped tightly in his left hand. He burst out of a cluster of young trees into a small clearing. Musket, the fur along his spine standing up straight, was barking like crazy. The boy jumped to one side of the dog, drawing his bow string back. When he saw what the wolf-dog was barking at, he laughed and lowered the arrow.

"Musket," he called, "you'd best leave that fellow alone."

Skunks grow big in the Rocky Mountains. This one was the fattest and biggest Scrapper John had seen in his entire fifteen years. And from the looks of things, it had listened to just about enough barking from Musket. The skunk shifted his stout body around gracefully. His white-striped tail arched high.

"Hey!" John shouted. "Musket, you're gonna git . . . !"

Scrapper John had underestimated the power and range of the old skunk. A stream of thick, amber liquid caught Musket in the side and chest and then hit Scrapper John.

He fell to the ground as if he'd been dropped by a punch, gasping and wheezing, his eyes streaming tears. Musket rolled wildly in the grass, yelping as if his tail were on fire. The skunk nonchalantly wandered off, undoubtedly returning to the meal of grubs that Musket had disturbed.

"Doggone you, Musket!" Scrapper John choked out. "Don't you know a skunk when you see one?" He rubbed at his eyes with the backs of his hands, trying to find his way back to the stream. Musket followed, slinking along and dropping every few moments to roll on the ground.

The boy's eyes were watering so badly he could barely see. The acid reek of the skunk spray made each breath a torture. "Musket, I'm gonna hang your hide on a tree, you knucklehead."

Scrapper John stumbled against a young tree and pushed it angrily out of his way. The tree, only a couple of inches in diameter, bent easily and snapped back to its normal position. Something gray and about the size of a small loaf of bread snapped loose from a branch, turned over once in the air, and thumped down in a patch of grass. A high-pitched, angry buzz filled the small clearing.

Scrapper John, grumbling to himself and still not able to see very well, didn't notice it at first. Musket, even though he had his own problems, did. He'd had a run-in with wasps as a pup and had never forgotten it. He rushed at his master, barking frantically.

"Musket!" Scrapper John roared. "What's wrong with you now? Ain't you done enough for one day?"

Musket threw himself at his master's legs, knocking the boy backward. Scrapper John's rump landed directly on the hive. His yell was loud enough to be heard in Mexico. When the wasps found Musket, the combination of the boy's yells and the howls of the dog could have carried to the moon.

Boy and dog raced back to the shore of the stream, where the mud next to the flowing water was black, thick, and cool. Scrapper John tore off his clothing and moccasins, still slapping at wasps. He dove into the mud as if it were a pool of cold water in the midst of a desert. Musket flipped over and rolled, digging his back and shoulders into the ooze.

When the wasp stings began to hurt less and the skunk stench seemed less unbearable, Scrapper John opened his eyes and looked over at Musket. The dog was buried in the mud next to him, with only his head above the surface. The

40

wolf-dog was staring at him intently. When John turned to him, Musket looked away, ashamed, and whined miserably. The mountain boy reached a hand out of the mud and scratched the dog's muzzle.

The corners of Scrapper John's mouth began to twitch. He burst into howls of laughter, his whole body shaking, drying mud cracking on his face and arms. When his laughter finally ended, he felt much better. Musket eyed him warily. Scrapper John noticed a wasp sting between the dog's eyes that looked like a small mountain growing out of the fur, and his laughter started all over again.

Eventually, hunger and boredom drove the boy and his dog from their mud bath. Scrapper John hauled his pants out of the mud where he'd buried them, but left his shirt for the time being. The skunk had missed his pants, and they didn't carry too much of the odor. Musket shook himself, throwing bits of wet mud in the air. He still smelled strongly, but the mud had sucked away much of the stink. The boy sat down and tugged on his moccasins, wincing in pain from the wasp stings on his arms and chest.

Scrapper John and Musket walked back through the woods to get Scrapper John's bow, making a very wide detour around the still-buzzing wasp hive. The sun was well past its midpoint for the day, and the woods were still. Scrapper John heard a rustling, thumping sound beyond the thicket where he and Musket had met the skunk. He held out his hand to stop Musket and listened.

41

Walking carefully, selecting the spot where each foot touched the ground, he crept to his bow. He notched the arrow and crouched, moving slowly forward as silent as a shadow. Using a bush for cover, he drew the bow and waited. His right hand began to tremble under the stress of the powerful bow, but he held the string tightly.

The steady, rhythmic thumping became louder. Seconds later, a hefty male turkey strode into sight, beating his wings against his sides. Two hen turkeys followed him almost shyly, clucking to themselves. The tom gobbled loudly at the hens and again beat his wings against his plump body. When the hens didn't move fast enough to suit him, he erupted into a series of angry gobbles.

Scrapper John unleashed the arrow. It was the last time the tom squabbled with his lady friends.

Back at the stream, Scrapper John started a fire, but it took a couple of hours to burn down to the coals needed to properly roast the turkey. The tom had been a big one, and there was plenty of meat. The boy wrapped the drumsticks, breast meat, and wings in the large leaves of a water plant. He coated the leaves thickly with mud and placed them on the coals, turning them with a pointed stick every so often. The smell of the roasting turkey was almost good enough to make the boy and dog forget about the scent of skunk that still hung heavily on them.

Later, gnawing at a steaming drumstick, Scrapper John was struck once more by the sensation that he was being watched. This time, he was more irritated than uneasy. Musket was no help. His fur reeked so badly of skunk he couldn't have smelled a moose if one had been standing next to him.

Scrapper John stood and looked up and down the stream. He saw nothing out of the ordinary and returned to his meal. The smoke from his fire drifted almost straight up in the still air. He had no reason to try to conceal himself or his fire. He had no argument with any Indians who might be passing by. Stone Pete had good relations with all the area tribes and so did the boy.

After they'd eaten, Scrapper John wrestled Musket back into the mud and coated the dog with the thick black ooze. Musket growled and lunged at the boy, catching him off balance. Scrapper John flopped in the mud on his back and came up laughing, grabbing at Musket. They rolled together in a friendly battle. Scrapper John's laughter was just as loud as Musket's barking.

Afterward, they sat together on the stream bank, covered with mud. Scrapper John dropped his arm over Musket's back. "Ain't neither one of us gonna be mistook for a spring flower." He laughed. "But we smell a sight better than we did earlier. Good thing the stream was here, partner. There's nothin' like black mud dryin' to suck up that skunk smell."

As the sun dropped below the tops of the trees, they moved closer to the embers of the fire for warmth. The heat helped dry the layer of mud that covered both of them. Scrapper John picked cakes of the dried dirt from Musket's coat. As he tossed one into the stream, he noticed that the water seemed to be flowing even faster than it had been earlier, and that it was spreading higher up the banks. That meant it had rained hard upstream that day. White foam bobbed on the rushing torrent, where it swirled past a sharp rock in the middle of the stream.

Scrapper John stared into the rushing water. A feeling of sadness swept over him as his mind drifted back to his father's death. Silently, he vowed that one day he'd make the one-eyed grizzly pay for killing Stone Pete. But that didn't change how much he missed his father. Stone Pete had once told John that there was nothing unmanly about crying. That comforted him when a tear trickled slowly down his cheek. More than anything, Scrapper John wanted to grow to be like his mountain man father.

The embers of the fire gave off heat like an oven. Scrapper John sat with his knees up, facing the fire. He folded his arms on the tops of his knees and lowered his head onto his sleeve. He was growing sleepy. At his side, Musket already slept, his paws moving as he dreamed. Soon, the mountain boy was also dozing comfortably, lulled to sleep by the warmth and the steady sound of rushing water.

A loud crack broke the evening quiet. Scrapper John's eyes snapped open. Musket was on his feet in a heartbeat, and Scrapper John was right next to him.

Then they heard someone scream. The boy and his dog raced down the banks of the stream toward the sound. The terror-filled scream began again but was cut in half by the racing torrent!

CHAPTER FIVE

For a moment, Scrapper John saw nothing but madly swirling water. Then his eyes swung to an oak tree further along the bank of the stream. Fresh yellow wood showed halfway up the trunk where a branch had broken off. It was in the water now, bobbing and turning as the current swept it toward Scrapper John and his dog. Suddenly, the head of a boy popped to the surface. Even in the murky light it was easy to see that his eyes were white with terror.

The boy disappeared underwater and then bobbed to the surface again. His choking and coughing could be heard even over the rush of the current. He saw Scrapper John standing on the shore, and for a single moment, the eyes of the two boys met. Then the stream broke the contact.

Scrapper John dashed back to the place where he'd dropped his sack and grabbed the coil of rope from it. He shook the loop at the end of the rope loose, swung it over his head, and rushed back to the edge of the stream, keeping his eyes on the sharp point of rock in the middle of the stream.

He made his first throw too quickly, and the loop bounced off the rock and dropped into the current. He hauled the rope back to shore. This time, he forced himself to move more slowly and keep his excitement under control. As he coiled the rope, the struggling boy came to the surface and grabbed at a boulder. The surface of the rock was wet and covered with moss, and the boy's fingers slipped from it in seconds. He was dragged under the muddy water again.

Scrapper John gauged the distance to the sharp rock carefully. Every instinct told him to hurry and make his throw, but this time, the throw had to be good. There wouldn't be another chance. The drowning boy would be swept away in the current.

Scrapper John put everything but the rock and his rope out of his mind. He twirled the loop over his head, making sure it opened properly. At exactly the right moment, he hurled the loop, following through as if he were throwing a ball. The lasso flashed out as straight as a well-aimed arrow and settled over the jagged point of rock.

Scrapper John whooped and ran to a thick oak well away from the stream. He wrapped the rest of the rope around the trunk and pulled it tight so there was a taut line of rope running across the stream just above the surface of the swirling water. He secured it with a fast pair of knots and ran to the stream. He dove into the rushing waters, holding the rope tightly, and worked himself hand over hand out into the current.

The fast-flowing water pulled and tugged at him, prying his hands away from the rope. He felt as if a strong man had taken hold of his legs and was trying to drag him under. Musket's barking caused Scrapper John to look back at the shore. The dog was set to launch himself into the water to follow his master.

"No, Musket! You stay! Stay, boy!" Scrapper John shouted.

Musket was as strong a swimmer as a timber wolf, but the swollen stream was far too powerful even for him. The wolf-dog jumped up and down the shore, whining and yelping, his eyes never leaving Scrapper John.

The dark-haired boy bobbed to the surface thirty feet away from Scrapper John. His mouth was open wide, and he coughed and spit water. Blood ran down the side of his face from a cut over his left eye. Scrapper John could see the boy was exhausted.

"I'll git you!" Scrapper John shouted with more confidence than he felt. When the boy was ten feet away, the water pulled at his legs and tugged him under the surface and out of sight again.

Scrapper John let go of the rope with one of his hands and put his head underwater, trying to locate the boy. It was impossible. The water was thick with grit. Just as he pushed his head to the surface, he saw the boy swirl toward him.

Scrapper John grabbed what he could, grabbing at the boy's clothing. His hand closed around a leather vest, but the current pulled it away from him. He lunged out, this time winding his fist into the boy's long black hair.

The shock of having his hair pulled seemed to bring new spirit to the exhausted youth. He clutched Scrapper John's forearm with both of his hands and kicked against the current. Inch by inch the two boys edged down the rope toward the shore.

The shore was so near Scrapper John was about to let out a victory whoop, when Musket howled. The rescued boy shouted and grabbed for a knife that he wore in a sheath on his belt.

"He ain't a wolf!" Scrapper John yelled into the boy's ear. "He's a dog! A dog!" It was clear to him now that this was an Indian boy, who didn't seem to understand what John was saying.

The boy held his knife above water with one hand and clutched the rope with the other. The shore was only a few feet away. Musket danced back and forth on the bank, barking wildly. Scrapper John hollered again, "He's a . . ."

Suddenly a log flew up from the rushing current of the stream and slammed into the side of the Indian's head. The boy let go of both the rope and Scrapper John, and was immediately pulled underwater. Scrapper John released his grip on the rope and dove after him. The log bobbed up and struck him on the head, too, driving him underwater. He came up almost onshore and scrambled for dry ground, yelling, "Musket! Git him, boy!"

The dog was in the water like a shot. Close to the shore the current didn't have the raw power it did midstream. Still, Musket had to use every ounce of his strength to keep from being swept away. He dove, his paws digging wildly in the muddy, raging stream. Scrapper John crawled ashore on his belly and pushed himself to his feet, gasping and choking.

He lurched back toward the stream, shouting, "Musket! Musket!" But the wolf-dog was nowhere to be seen.

Scrapper John was about to dive back in when Musket's head suddenly bobbed to the surface a few feet from shore. His long white teeth were clamped tightly on the leather belt around the Indian boy's waist. He battled against the force of the water until his feet touched sand. Scrapper John reached forward and got his hands under the boy's arms. He dragged the unconscious Indian boy onto the bank of the stream. Musket followed, his chest heaving with his heavy panting.

"Good boy, Musket," Scrapper John said, meaning it with his whole heart. "That ol' skunk an' them bees don't mean nothin', partner. What counts is that you just saved this kid's life. I'm so proud of you I could bust wide open."

Musket's tail swung back and forth. Water ran in streams from his coat. His tongue hung limply from his mouth as he continued to pant, but his eyes showed that he understood what his master was saying.

Scrapper John hefted the barely conscious boy in his arms and carried him to the fire. The embers were finally dying. He put the youth down and shoved his sack of gear under the boy's head. The Indian coughed and moaned but didn't fully awaken. Scrapper John collected an armful of dry branches and brush and dumped it on the embers. The fire flared, and soon the heat brought the other boy to consciousness. He opened his eyes and coughed, spitting muddy water. His dark eyes focused slowly. He pushed himself up.

"Are you okay?" Scrapper John asked. "I thought you was a goner there for a minute."

The Indian boy's face was blank. Obviously he didn't understand English.

"When that log come along and hit you, it whacked me a good one, too." This time Scrapper John spoke in the Nez Perce language, which he had learned from his mother as a little boy. The Indian boy still didn't understand.

"Sorry," Scrapper John said, switching back to English. He held his hands up in front of himself with his palms toward his chest.

The Indian boy flashed a smile. He held his hands in front, exactly as Scrapper John had done.

The sign language both boys were about to use was far older than either of them. Since the various tribes spoke in different languages that had little in common with one another, it was necessary for them to develop a language all could understand. It was common for the person doing the signing to speak in his own language as he did so. That way, spoken words could be learned by the other party. Stone Pete had taught signing to Scrapper John as soon as the boy was old enough to form the symbols with his hands and fingers.

"I am Seeks The Far Sky," the Indian signed. "You have saved my life, and I thank you. I will soon give you a great gift."

"I am Scrapper John. My dog is Musket," Scrapper John signed saying the names out loud, then repeating them.

The mountain boy also knew that the Indian tribes were very proud and always repaid whatever debts they had, or thought they had. He thought for a moment before moving his hands.

"My great gift is that you are alive and here to share my fire. What tribe are you from?" To sign "tribe," Scrapper John spread his arms wide and then brought them slowly together, hugging himself.

"I am a Blackfoot," the boy signed. "I am traveling alone." The sign for alone was to clench one's fist with the first finger raised, to show a one. "We have been traveling in the same direction for two days."

Scrapper John laughed. "So it was you watching me an' Musket—" he started saying out loud. Then he remembered the Indian boy couldn't understand him, and he started signing again. "Sometimes I felt someone was watching me."

The boy smiled and made more signs. "Yes, sometimes I watched. But I did not intend to hurt you. I am on a journey to the Valley of the Spotted Horses. I will catch and train one of the spotted horses and take him to my home. Then I will be a warrior."

Scrapper John was fascinated. "Where is this valley?" he asked with his hands.

The Indian boy's smile faltered for a moment but returned quickly. He turned his palms upward in front of his body, meaning, "I don't know." Then he added, "It is near where the sun sets. I will find it." He used the first two fingers of his right hand to symbolize legs walking. He was asking, "Where are you going?"

Scrapper John signed that he was headed to visit Dark Eagle Walking, of the Nez Perce tribe.

Seeks The Far Sky's face showed that he recognized the name. He frowned angrily as he signed, "The Nez Perce are cowards, and they eat beetles."

Scrapper John flapped his right hand as if to clear the air, which meant, "You are wrong." Then he added, still signing, "My mother was a Nez Perce. Her name was Silent Fox."

All Indian tribes had great respect for their mothers. To insult the mother of another man could easily lead to a fight to the death. Seeks The Far Sky signed, "I am very sorry for what I said. But the Blackfeet and the Nez Perce are enemies."

When he made the symbol for enemies—banging the fronts of his closed fists together in front of his chest—he winced in pain. His knuckles were scraped and bleeding from the rocks in the stream.

"We are not enemies," Scrapper John signed back.

"We are friends," Seeks The Far Sky answered with his hands.

The fire burned away the dry branches Scrapper John had piled on it. He noticed the Indian boy shiver. Night had fallen, and the air was cool. Seeks The Far Sky coughed, caught his breath, and coughed again. Scrapper John's face showed his concern. The Indian boy suddenly looked dazed, as if he'd just woken from a long sleep.

"What is it?" Scrapper John asked aloud, for a moment forgetting the language barrier. "Are you hurt?"

Seeks The Far Sky held his head in his hands for a long moment. Scrapper John and Musket stood next to him nervously, wondering what was wrong. Other than the cuts and scrapes, the boy didn't appear to have been harmed by his fight with the stream. But he sure wasn't acting healthy. Finally, the dark-haired boy looked up at Scrapper John. When he lifted his hands, they trembled. "I am very tired," he signed slowly. "I will be better after I sleep."

"Sure," Scrapper John said aloud without signing again. "Do you want some jerky before you go to sleep?" he asked.

Seeks The Far Sky shook his head and signed, "I need sleep more than food."

Scrapper John sprang like a mountain cat, dragging Seeks The Far Sky to his feet by one arm and a handful of his hair.

"You're a fake!" he yelled into the Indian boy's face. "You're trying to trick me. I ain't no dummy, an' I ain't gonna let you git away with it!"

Seeks The Far Sky pushed at Scrapper John's chest with his hands, trying to free himself.

Scrapper John stepped back, keeping his hands up to block a punch—or to throw one. "Start talkin', or start swingin'!" he snarled.

CHAPTER SIX

Musket started barking frantically and ran to his master's side, the fur along his spine standing up like porcupine quills. Scrapper John readied himself for a fight.

Seeks The Far Sky stepped forward as if he were about to attack. Suddenly, the Indian boy's eyes rolled up inside his head, and he began to slump. Scrapper John caught him just as he crumpled to the ground.

This time, Scrapper John knew there was no trick involved. The boy's face had turned a chalky gray. He eased Seeks The Far Sky down next to the dying camp fire. He wished he'd collected lots of wood. Now, he had to leave the boy alone to gather more. He was sure some good food would help, but he and Musket had feasted on the turkey, and there was none left. It was a dark night, and there were clouds in the sky. Hunting would be difficult.

Scrapper John made a decision. It might take some time, but he had to find food. He looked down at the Indian boy and snapped his fingers. Musket dashed to his side.

"You stay and watch Seeks The Far . . . dang! That name's a mouthful! Musket—you stay an' watch . . . uhh . . . Seeks. Nah—that don't sound right, neither. How 'bout Sky? Sure! That sounds jist right! Musket—you watch Sky real close, hear?"

Musket moved beside the sleeping boy. Scrapper John covered Sky with his oilcloth, scratched Musket's back, and strode into the darkness.

There were plenty of dead branches in the woods near the camp. Scrapper John built up the fire and then checked to make sure Sky was sleeping as comfortably as possible. He picked up his bow and quiver and set off into the dark. When he returned to the camp half an hour later, he carried a possum slung over his shoulder.

In minutes he had the meat wrapped in leaves and the leaves covered with mud. When the smell of roasting meat began to waft through the air, Sky stirred, opened his eyes, and sat up slowly.

"Now how 'bout talkin' some English, 'stead of pretending you don't know any," Scrapper John said firmly, eyeing the boy.

"You are right," Sky said. "I know some English, but it has been a long time since I used it."

"Why'd you try to trick me? Me an' Musket jist saved your hide."

"Because I was taught never to trust the

white man. Even after you and Biscuit pulled me . . ."

Scrapper John howled with laughter. "It's Musket, not Biscuit. An' your English ain't bad at all. See, you gave yourself away when I asked out loud if you wanted some jerky. You shook your head, an' then you signed you wasn't hungry. But if you didn't know English, you wouldn't have known I asked that. Who learned you white talk?"

"The men who trap on our lands. The mountain men. Do you know of them?"

Scrapper John smiled proudly. "I sure do. My pa was one of 'em."

"Why do you say 'was?'"

"'Cause my pa is dead."

Sky waited for Scrapper John to explain. When he didn't, Sky said, "I am making this trip because I had a spirit vision. It is what I must do to become a warrior."

Scrapper John was quiet for a long time. "My pa's death is the reason for me goin' to Dark Eagle Walking." He was quiet again for a moment. "My pa said things happen for a reason. I wonder if there's some reason you an' me met up after my father died."

Sky's face was just as serious as Scrapper John's. "There must be. We said we were friends. Maybe that's why." Sky coughed, and he turned pale again. He coughed so hard that he was left gasping for air.

Scrapper John crouched next to Sky. "Somethin' ain't right with you, Sky. You got somethin' bad

58

goin' on inside your lungs or somethin'. Look, my grandfather, Dark Eagle Walking, is a medicine man. Come with me. He'll fix you up."

Sky's face was pale, but his eyes were blazing. "Never! A Blackfoot doesn't go to Nez Perce for anything! There's nothing wrong. . . . He was interrupted again by his own coughing.

Scrapper John stabbed a sharp stick into a piece of leaf-wrapped possum meat and took it from the fire. He set it down next to Sky.

"I got an idea," he said. "You come with me to Dark Eagle Walking, and I'll go with you to that place where the spotted horses are. You ain't gonna be no good travelin' or bustin' horses till you're better. An' Dark Eagle Walking can make you better."

Sky began coughing again. When he stopped, he was out of breath and his face was deathly pale.

"I will come." He signed because he couldn't find the breath to speak. "Together we will find the spotted horses."

"Dang right we will," Scrapper John said. "Now, you git some food into you an' then try some sleep."

Sky peeled the leaf wrapper from a piece of possum meat. "It is hard for me to go to the Nez Perce for anything, even if Dark Eagle Walking is part of your family."

"It'd be even harder for you to travel with that cough of yours. An' how do you think you'd do if you was settin' on one of them wild horses an' you got all weak like you just done?"

Sky gnawed on the steaming meat. "What you say makes tents. But I . . ."

"Tents?" Scrapper John laughed. "You mean *sense*."

Sky shook his head slowly from side to side, grinning. "Your English is a funny way to talk. We Blackfeet have simple words for things. You have words that sound the same but mean different things. I have seen what white men call writing, and it is lazy. It looks like the tracks of birds in the sand."

Scrapper John was confused for a moment. Then he smiled. "You're right about writing, it don't make no sense to me, neither. I can read a little an' write my name good, but . . ." Scrapper John laughed. "Like my pa used to say, 'You don't have to understand what makes the sun hot for it to keep you warm.' "

"What does that mean? What does the sun have to do with talking English? Everyone knows that the sun and the moon and the stars have their own tongues to speak to one another, but it is not English."

"No, you're missing the point, Sky. See, a man don't have to understand the sun. All he has to do is feel how warm it is. Nobody asks no questions about it. It's jist there. Get it?"

"No. It sounds like a story Blackfeet mothers tell to babies."

Scrapper John sighed. "Let's chow down an' git some shuteye, Sky. We can get movin' at first light."

The next day, they traveled more slowly than

Scrapper John was used to, because Sky tired very quickly. Musket seemed to take to the Indian boy as well as Scrapper John did. Musket had always been a friendly dog, but he was devoted only to Scrapper John. Now, for some reason, the dog walked next to Sky for a few minutes at a time before going back to Scrapper John's side. Both of the boys noticed this. Neither said anything, but it made them both feel good.

Scrapper John brought down a fat quail with an arrow the morning of their second day together.

"You shoot well, John," Sky said. "You were a little high on that shoot, but it was still good."

"High!" Scrapper John exclaimed. "That shot wasn't an inch high! It brought the bird down, didn't it? Why, I can shoot a speck of dust off a flea's eyelash from three miles away!"

Sky folded his arms across his chest, a smile playing at the corners of his mouth. "We Blackfeet are the best hunters on earth. I could shoot a bow before I could walk. My eye is like that of the hawk. White men have guns, because they cannot use a bow like the Blackfeet."

Scrapper John handed his bow and quiver to Sky. "Seems like I hear a little shootin' match comin' up. Git the feel of my bow." He tugged his red bandanna from his pocket. "This can be our target. I'll walk out to that little oak out there, an' we'll just see who can shoot an' who can't."

Scrapper John walked to a small tree about fifteen yards away and looked back at Sky, who was rubbing dust between his palms and on his fingers. The Indian boy waved him further and

61

picked up the bow. Scrapper John turned and kept on walking, stopping at another tree a full fifty yards from where Sky stood. He used the rough bark of the tree to hold the bandanna in place. As he walked back, the Indian boy tested his bow.

"Not a bad bow," Sky said. "Your arrows are good ones. Did you make them?"

"My pa showed me how. He helped me make the bow, too. He was the best shot I've ever seen. He fought in the Great War usin' guns an' cannons an' all, but he made an oath to himself an' to my ma. After the war he promised he was never goin' to shoot a rifle or pistol at another livin' thing for the rest of his life."

Seeks The Far Sky looked puzzled. "Will not an arrow make a living thing as dead as a white man's bullet will?"

"Sure," Scrapper John answered. "But my pa seen so much death caused by guns he couldn't stand to ever pick one up again. And at some of them battles, both sides was fillin' cannons with chains an' stones an' jist about anything they could find. Sure, an arrow can kill a man, but my pa told me them cannons an' scatterguns they was usin' were killin' ten or twenty or even more at a shot."

"Is not one man's life as important as ten or twenty?" Seeks The Far Sky asked.

"Sure it is," Scrapper John answered. "But this was a thing that my pa promised himself. It's jist somethin' he had to do. An' I made the same promise five years ago, so I ain't gonna break it."

The boys were silent for a moment, their eyes locked on each other's. Sky broke the spell by turning toward the target. The red bandanna looked very small when it was fifty yards away.

"You go first," Scrapper John said. "Take your choice of my arrows."

Sky selected two arrows from the quiver. He held each one up in front of his eyes and sighted down the shaft to make sure they were perfectly straight. He licked the forefinger of his right hand and held it up. A slightly cooler feel on the skin on one side meant a little breeze was coming from his right side. He notched an arrow, drew the bow back with a grunt, held that position for a heartbeat, and let the arrow fly. It slammed into the tree with a *thunk* an inch below the bottom of the bandanna.

Seeks The Far Sky handed the bow to Scrapper John, obviously pleased but without saying anything. Scrapper John drew back the string and fired in one smooth motion. His arrow jammed deep into the wood right next to Sky's.

When he handed the bow back to Sky, the boy said, "You take your second shot."

A moment later, Scrapper John's second arrow quivered in the tree, an inch above the top of the bandanna. He gave the bow to his friend.

Sky fired his second arrow as quickly as Scrapper John had, his movements smooth and sure. The arrow struck the tree an inch to the side of Scrapper John's. There was a long silence. Then the boys looked at each other. Suddenly, the quiet woods was filled with their laughter.

Sky tossed the bow back to Scrapper John. "Friends like us don't need contests. One day I miss; one day you miss. It don't make no difference. We . . ."

A spell of coughing forced Sky to bend over, clutching at his chest. His face was suddenly slick with sweat. Scrapper John bit his lip and watched his friend gasping for breath. He felt completely helpless. They rested until Sky felt clearheaded enough to walk and then set out at a slower pace. Toward evening, Sky began looking about nervously.

"We must be getting near the home of the Nez Perce," he said. "I have a feeling we're being watched."

"I've felt it, too," Scrapper John told him. "Almost like I did when you was followin' me an' Musket." He grinned. "Not all of the Nez Perce know me, but you can bet they know we're here. We're real close to the camp. The guards probably been watchin' us for half the day already."

Musket was sniffing the air. "Look," Sky said. "He knows we're not alone out here, too. I hope all they do is keep watching. They have no reason to put an arrow in you, but I am a Blackfoot. Our tribes have been enemies for many years, long before I was born."

"If they wanted our hair for their tepees, they'd have took it when we first got close an' the guards started watchin' us. You got the wrong idea 'bout them, Sky. The Nez Perce are real friendly. Maybe there was bad blood between some of your older warriors and the Nez Perce, but that's all over."

As he spoke, an arrow stabbed into an oak inches from Scrapper John's face. Another hissed past Sky's forehead. Then, horrible whoops and shrieks shattered the quiet woods. Musket barked fiercely. Indian warriors ran from the trees, holding spears and knives, and coming straight at the two boys!

CHAPTER SEVEN

There were a dozen or more young warriors surrounding them, all of them two or three years older than Scrapper John and Sky. Some had their knives clutched in their hands, while others had spears. Three held arrows drawn back in their bows and aimed at the two boys. Their eyes were cold and hard.

Musket snarled at the warriors, ready to attack but not moving from his master's side.

"Hold on, darn it," Scrapper John exclaimed, in the language of the Nez Perce Indians. "I'm . . ."

"Quiet!" A warrior yelled. "You are white, and this other one is Blackfoot," he snarled. "That's all we need to know! Get their weapons," he ordered the other braves. Sky watched uncertainly, straining to make sense of the unfamiliar language.

In moments, Scrapper John's and Sky's sheath

knives and the bow and arrows were in the hands of the warriors. Scrapper John held Musket back with a quick command. The wolf-dog growled, his fangs dripping saliva. A rope snaked out from the circle of Nez Perce, with a lasso falling around his head. Musket was suddenly on his back. The poor wolf-dog howled and whined as he was dragged through the dirt and grass. Five of the warriors jumped onto the dog, and in seconds he was tied helplessly, able to do nothing but snarl.

"We would have killed him," the leader said. "But we can see he is half wolf. Instead, we will let him live. He will be a good guard for us. Now, we will show you how we treat unwanted visitors."

Scrapper John and Seeks The Far Sky stood side by side, their fists ready, waiting for the charge. The Nez Perce laughed as they closed in on the boys. The ones carrying spears were slightly ahead of the others and swinging the spear shafts.

Sky jumped back but grimaced in pain when the wood shaft grazed his knee. Scrapper John tried to grab the spear, but the warrior was too quick. He reversed his swing and tore skin from Scrapper John's knuckles with a rapid blow.

Scrapper John knew that trying to tell the warriors who he was was foolish. If they'd known him, none of this would be happening. If he tried to tell them, they'd see it as cowardice, and that would only make things worse. He crouched slightly with his fists up, waiting. Next to him, Sky did the same.

The leader pulled one of the spear carriers back by his shoulders and stepped into his place. Then, so quickly that Sky didn't have a chance, the warrior buried his fist in Sky's stomach. Scrapper John swung at the brave but missed. One of the warriors raised his spear over his head and swung it with all his strength at Scrapper John's legs.

This time, it wasn't a glancing blow. He tried to jump, but he was not fast enough. When it hit Scrapper John's leg, the force of the impact threw him to the ground. Next to him, he heard Sky grunt as another punch found its mark.

A warrior dove on Scrapper John, pinning him to the ground. Another aimed his moccasin at the boy's chest. Scrapper John couldn't move. He heard Sky being slammed to the ground beside him.

Then, a yelp of pain made the warriors freeze.

A short, very heavy Nez Perce woman with her hair in shiny black pigtails had appeared from out of the blue. She had a tight grip on the long hair of one of the warriors and held the young man at arm's length, kicking him soundly and solidly in the rear end. She was wearing laced leather boots with thick, hard toes. With her other hand, she swung a switch made from the branch of a birch tree. It whistled through the air and made a sharp *crack!* when it struck the young brave's skin.

The other Nez Perce boys scrambled away as

if a rampaging buffalo was after them. Scrapper John had a clear view from the ground, and even through his fear and pain he had to laugh.

"I'll show you boys how to attack!" the squaw bellowed in a foghorn voice. "Here! And here! And here, you brave warriors!" Each of her words was accompanied by a good hard kick. The young braves fled before the short woman's charge, using their hands to shield their heads from the switch. She let go of the first warrior's hair after giving him one final kick.

"Nez Perce do not fight ten against one, you slimy egg-stealing lizards! Your fathers will know of this before the sun sets! Run, you toothless snakes!" she shouted after the fleeing boys.

The woman looked down at Scrapper John and whooped in joy. The mountain boy jumped to his feet and answered the whoop with one of his own just as the squaw pulled him close in a bear hug.

"Aunt Big!" He gasped as she squeezed the air from his lungs. "You showed up at exactly the right time."

The woman let him go and stood back, beaming with joy. "Those boys cause me shame, Scrapper John. Even if they didn't know you are the son of my sister, they should not have attacked you without cause." She looked over at Sky, who stood off to one side. "And who is your Blackfoot friend?"

Scrapper John turned to his friend. "Seeks The Far Sky, this is my aunt, Shakes A Big Fist. She was my ma's sister."

Sky signed a greeting and then gestured to say,

"I am honored to meet you. Just as my friend Scrapper John said, you came just in time to drive the warriors from us. I thank you."

"Warriors!" She spat, her hands moving rapidly in sign language. "Those were maggots!"

Then she hugged Sky as hard and as long as she'd hugged Scrapper John. Sky grinned at his friend over Shakes A Big Fist's head. It was easy, since the short woman stood barely higher than their chests.

When the hug was over, Shake a Big Fist's round face was gleaming with happiness. "Not often do I hug two handsome men in the same day."

A low growl sounded behind the boys.

"Musket!" Scrapper John exclaimed. He ran toward the sounds on the other side of a clump of bushes and quickly untied the unhappy wolf-dog. Together, they dashed back to where Sky was waiting with Shakes A Big Fist.

"Now John, tell me of your father and why you have come without him. Is my tepee so bad he was afraid to visit?" the Indian woman asked. Without waiting for an answer, she motioned the boys to follow her and started off down a trail that led into the woods. "But, come! We'll walk as we talk. Dark Eagle will be so happy to see you, John! But—tell me of Stone Pete. A piece of my heart has always been with him. Why did he not come to visit, along with you and Seeks The Far Sky?"

She laughed happily. "Stone Pete would have

eaten those young pups for breakfast—and their fathers, too, for not raising their boys to be men."

Scrapper John looked at Sky, and without saying anything, the Indian boy knew that his friend wanted to speak alone with his aunt, to tell her of his father's death. He stopped, and Scrapper John and his aunt went on ahead.

Scrapper John put his arm around Shakes A Big Fist's broad shoulders and spoke with his face close to hers. The Nez Perce woman's words of happiness changed to a cry of shock and sorrow.

Seeks The Far Sky looked away. The Blackfeet, like all Native Americans, believed very strongly in an afterlife. Death, to them, was not an end but a beginning. Still, all people felt the pain of losing someone they loved very deeply.

Shakes A Big Fist hurried on ahead to speak with Dark Eagle Walking and other friends of Stone Pete's in the tribe. Scrapper John motioned Sky up to his side. They waited under an oak tree in the forest, giving the Nez Perce woman time to tell the tribe about Stone Pete's death. After a half an hour, the boys began walking again.

Dark Eagle Walking and a group of Nez Perce warriors and women met the boys when they reached the edge of the Indian village. Dark Eagle was tall, and his body still showed that he'd once been a young and powerful warrior. His hair was a pure, snowy white, and his face was lined with wrinkles. His eyes were chestnut and burned with his spirit. Dark Eagle Walking

71

embraced Scrapper John and held him close for a long moment. Into the boy's ear he said quietly, "Stone Pete Lewis lives on in his son, Scrapper John."

"And in the hearts of Dark Eagle Walking and his other Nez Perce friends," Scrapper John answered.

Dark Eagle Walking turned to look at Seeks The Far Sky.

"Welcome," he signed. "It is a great honor to have a Blackfoot warrior in our camp." He spoke loudly as he signed, so that the other Nez Perce knew that Seeks The Far Sky was a guest and not to be bothered in any way.

Dogs and children raced around the two strangers, pushing to get a close look at the white boy and the Blackfoot. Musket ran through the crowd, barking and jumping to protect his master. Then Musket stood next to Scrapper John, his lips curling back over his fangs whenever one of the Indian dogs came too close.

The warm, inviting scent of venison, vegetables, and spices wafted in the air. Not far away, a huge black stew pot was suspended from a tripod of stout shafts over a white-hot bed of coals. Dark Eagle Walking smiled when he noticed both boys gazing at the stew pot. He put an arm over each of their shoulders and guided them toward his tepee.

"We shall eat after we've talked," he said.

Scrapper John looked at Musket and snapped his fingers, pointing to a spot next to Dark Eagle

Walking's tepee. Musket went there and sat, his wolflike eyes peering about the camp.

Since only one of the three flaps of the tepee was open, the light inside was murky and smelled of the pungent, well-tanned deer and mountain lion hides that were spread across the dirt floor. A headdress made of eagle feathers hung from a tepee crosspiece, its tail of feathers reaching to the floor. A spear, a small drum, and many small sacks tied with rawhide thongs had been placed next to the door. The sacks contained medicines, spices, and herbs Dark Eagle Walking used to treat sickness among the Nez Perce.

Scrapper John and Sky were careful not to sit themselves directly between Dark Eagle Walking and the tepee doorway, which was a sign of disrespect. They sat cross-legged to one side, facing the older man. Neither boy spoke. They waited for the old Nez Perce medicine man to begin the conversation. This, too, was a sign of respect.

"What will you do now?" Dark Eagle Walking asked Scrapper John, signing as he spoke so that Sky would understand as well.

"I figure I'll go to the Valley of the Spotted Horses with my friend Sky, here, grandfather. We're gonna catch an' train a couple of them. Sky has to bring one back to his tribe to prove he's a warrior. I'm goin' 'cause I need a horse, an' 'cause me an' Sky are friends."

The medicine man looked gravely from boy to boy. "I can see friendship in your eyes. It is good. But Scrapper John, you know that you are welcome to stay with us and live with us if you choose to do so." His eyes locked with Scrapper John's. "You are of my blood and of my family."

The boy smiled at Dark Eagle Walking. "I been thinkin' some on what I am an' where I belong since Pa died." He shook his head. "Them young men who met me an' Sky figured we was 'bout as welcome here as a rattler at breakfast. I ain't real sure how the white people will see me, neither." He held his hands out in front of him in the dim light. "See, my skin is kinda between my pa's an' my ma's, but I ain't one or the other, really. I'm kind of a mix, like Musket's a mix of wolf an' dog." He shook his head again. "Hard to say where I belong."

Dark Eagle Walking held Scrapper John's eyes with his own. "It is a man's heart that tells him what he is and who he is, not the color of his skin. The color of a man's skin is no more important than how tall he is or how he chooses to worship the Great Spirit."

The old Indian sighed and thought for several moments. "This trip you will make with Seeks The Far Sky will be very good for both of you. I can feel that within myself, and I know it to be true." He closed his eyes and rocked slightly back and forth in his cross-legged position on the skins. "I see you on a spotted horse that is as black as the darkest night, with spots of white on his rump. He is a fine horse. I see your friend on a tall red horse with spots that are like the snow."

Dark Eagle Walking's eyes popped open and looked at the two boys. "I know of the Valley of the Spotted Horses—and I know of the danger from the fanged ones that hang over the canyon."

"Danger from fanged ones? What do you mean?" Scrapper John asked.

"It is said no man has taken a horse from that canyon. There is only one way out on horseback, and that is through a narrow pass that is alive with the fanged ones in numbers that are almost impossible to believe. It is said that the buzzing of their rattles sounds like hail striking a tepee during a storm, and that their hissing is louder than the wind."

Scrapper John glanced at Sky. "You didn't say nothin' 'bout no rattlers," he said. "It don't make no difference to me if it don't to you, but you should have told me about all them snakes."

Sky began to answer but instead raised a hand to his mouth to cover a cough. The color left his face in seconds. He suddenly pushed himself frantically to his feet, his hands clutching at his throat and then banging on his chest. He bent forward at the waist, and a series of coughs shook his body.

Scrapper John jumped to his feet, but he was a heartbeat too late. Sky fell, and he slammed down onto a buffalo robe spread on the dirt floor of the tepee. His eyes turned up inside his head, so that only the ghostly whites showed, and he lay perfectly still.

CHAPTER EIGHT

Dark Eagle Walking was at Sky's side at a bound, moving faster than Scrapper John had believed possible for an elderly person. The medicine man stretched Sky out full length on the buffalo robe, tilting the boy's head back slightly. Scrapper John watched, trembling.

"What . . . what's wrong with Sky?" he stuttered.

Dark Eagle Walking selected several of the small sacks from the pile near the door and loosened the thong holding one of the bags closed.

"Get Shakes A Big Fist, and tell her to make sure the lodge is heated!" he said sharply to Scrapper John. "I have no time to answer your questions!"

"But . . . but . . ."

"Now!" Dark Eagle Walking bellowed so loud that Scrapper John jumped. He rushed out of the tepee in search of Shakes A Big Fist.

Dark Eagle Walking pressed his ear to Sky's

chest. He nodded to himself and took a pinch of reddish gray powder from the sack. He spat on the powder to make it sticky and rolled it into a little ball as large as a pebble. He eased the ball into Sky's mouth so it would dissolve on his tongue. By the time Scrapper John stood inside the tepee again, Sky's breathing was far more normal.

"Shakes A Big Fist is making the lodge ready, grandfather," Scrapper John said.

"Good. Now, help me with your friend. It will not take long to heat the stones."

"Heat stones? How will hot rocks help Sky?"

Dark Eagle Walking wiped sweat from Sky's face with a piece of brightly colored cloth. "Your friend has a tightness in his chest that is not from his muscles but from his lungs, which allow him to breathe. The lodge is a tepee made with skins crossing over one another so that no air can enter or escape from inside of it. Stones are heated in a hot fire and taken inside. The heat is as dry as a desert wind. When water is sprinkled on the stones, warm clouds fill the air. I add herbs and the dust of weeds to that cloud, and the boy will breathe them. The cough will leave him, and so will his breathing problems. You, too, must rest in the lodge, Scrapper John. Your friend may have passed on the bad spirits which have entered him. Come! We must hurry!"

Scrapper John lifted Sky, grunting with the effort. Just then, two braves entered the tepee. Dark Eagle talked to them in Nez Perce for a moment. One of them, a full foot taller than

Scrapper John, took Sky from him and cradled the Blackfoot boy in his arms as easily as a mother holds a newborn baby. He carried Sky outside, while Scrapper John and his grandfather followed.

The sweat lodge stood outside the camp. As they drew close to it, the scent of burning pine filled the still air. The tepee itself was much smaller than Dark Eagle Walking's, and its exterior was brightly decorated with paintings of buffalo, deer, wolves, mountain cats, and other wild creatures. In front of the tepee was a fire of white-hot coals, filled with stones as big as pumpkins. Shakes A Big Fist was using a stick to push the stones from the fire and roll them into the entrance of the sweat lodge.

For some reason, Musket tried to block Scrapper John's way with his body, whining sharply. Dark Eagle Walking looked at the wolf-dog.

"He smells the scent of dried buffalo blood being burned in the fire, and it frightens him," the old medicine man said. "Don't worry—there is nothing to fear."

The brave carrying Sky set him down on a pile of hides. Scrapper John helped Dark Eagle Walking undress Sky and then took off his own clothes. It was quite dark inside the lodge. Hot rocks were piled in the center, and the earth floor was littered with fresh mountain sage. The fur had been removed from the tanned skins, and moisture glistened on them. Scrapper John sat next to Sky.

Sky's eyes fluttered open. He looked about, saw

where he was, and tried to smile. Already, he was beginning to sweat.

"I am glad you have brought me to a sweat lodge," he said to Dark Eagle Walking, who crouched by the entrance. Then he closed his eyes and settled back on the hides.

Dark Eagle Walking smiled down at the Blackfoot boy and then at Scrapper John. "I will be back to awaken you and Seeks The Far Sky when you've been in the lodge long enough to chase the bad spirits out of yourselves."

Scrapper John stretched out on a hide on the other side of the pile of hot stones. "I ain't gonna go to sleep, but I'll stay in here as long as you say, grandfather."

"You will sleep, my boy," Dark Eagle Walking said.

Scrapper John flicked a bead of sweat off his forehead with his finger. "I sure don't mean to sass you, but I ain't about to go to sleep. I'll keep a sharp eye on Sky an' come runnin' if anything goes wrong."

Four hours later Dark Eagle Walking and Shakes A Big Fist entered the sweat lodge with deerskin robes over their arms. Scrapper John and Seeks The Far Sky were both fast asleep.

Shakes A Big Fist nudged Scrapper John's shoulder. "Time to get up, sleepy John." She laughed. "Your grandfather told me you swore you would not doze off. We knew better."

Scrapper John rolled over on his side without waking.

Dark Eagle Walking shook Sky's shoulder

lightly. The Indian boy's eyes popped open. He took in a long, deep breath of the steamy air and smiled up at the Nez Perce medicine man. "I feel like you have cleansed my body and my spirit. Your lodge works as well as those of my people, the Blackfeet."

"Someday," Dark Eagle Walking answered, "I hope our tribes can talk to one another the way we talk right now, my young friend."

On the other side of the tepee, Auntie Big was still trying to rouse Scrapper John from his dreams.

Dinner was a special meal, in honor of hunters who had returned to the village while Scrapper John and Sky slept in the sweat lodge, and in honor of the boys, too.

Shakes A Big Fist brought the boys their food. Large chunks of boiled venison swam in a savory stew of vegetables and spices that was almost as thick as gravy. They used chunks of flat corn bread to sop up the rich liquid. Both boys ate as if they'd been starved for weeks. Even Musket feasted on pieces of venison covered with gravy. For dessert, the Nez Perce women had made a pudding from red raspberries, bits of dried apple, and honey.

Dark Eagle Walking sat between the boys as they ate. When the meal was finished, he asked the two boys to come to his tepee. They followed him through the camp and stood aside to let him enter first. A small pot of tallow burned with a low flame, giving plenty of light inside the tent.

When they were seated, Dark Eagle Walking reached behind his stack of medicine bags and handed a supple leather pouch to each boy. The pouches were small enough to fit nicely in their palms. They had been sewn all the way around, so that they couldn't be opened without being cut.

"I have made these for you while you slept. Into each I put things that will help you in your search for the Valley of the Spotted Horses. Each one holds a pinch of soil from this camp to help you to return safely here. Yours, Scrapper John, holds the tooth of a mountain wolf. Sky, yours has a tooth from a grizzly bear. And, in each I've put a venom tooth from one of the fanged ones. The venom teeth will keep you safe from those who live in the valley where the spotted horses run free."

The boys took the bags from Dark Eagle's hands. Then the old man handed them beaded thongs to wear around their necks, showing them how to thread the thongs through holes in the medicine pouches.

"Wear these until you are safe and far away from the valley. Then you must burn the medicine pouches and, when you are on the backs of the spotted horses you will capture, throw the ashes to the winds to thank the Spirits. Will you do that?"

"Of course we will, Grandfather," Scrapper John promised.

"It is a great honor to receive this good medicine from Dark Eagle Walking," said Sky.

Dark Eagle Walking pushed aside one of the

buffalo robes on the floor of the tepee, revealing smooth, sandy soil. He used the tip of his finger to draw in the sand.

"Here is the village. Follow the path of the sun as it sets to the spot where the hills turn to mountains. Seek a great wall of stone that sparkles like water in the sun. When you see that, you will need only to cross a river to begin your climb into the valley."

"Is it much of a climb, Grandfather?" Scrapper John asked.

"Yes. It is long and hard. Our legend says that the Spirits created the mountain that leads to the valley to keep the spotted horses safe."

He hesitated for a moment and then went on. "It is the same Spirits who placed the fanged ones in great numbers to keep any men from taking the spotted horses from the valley."

"Have any of the horses ever gotten out?" Sky asked.

"The Spirits have allowed a few to be taken out by great warriors, and it was those horses that began the breed called Appaloosa by white men. A sign that a horse is a true Appaloosa is the white that goes completely around each of his eyes. No other horse has such a mark. The Appaloosa is the horse that the Spirits ride in their home in the sky."

"Please, Grandpa, tell me some more about the climb and about the rattlesnakes," Scrapper John asked.

"The valley is big, with a river of cold water passing through it. The mountain that leads to the valley does not have white hair, because it is not high enough. But it is steep and dangerous, and the winds do not like it, so they howl and moan all day and night. With courage, you and Sky can climb it. This I know in my heart."

Dark Eagle Walking drew a long, narrow winding line in the sand. He poked his finger in the sand many times to represent rocks and boulders.

"The fanged ones live under the rocks in this pass," he said. "It is the only way out of the valley. They live on coyotes and birds, and sun themselves on the rocks and increase their numbers. It will be up to you to decide how you will bring your horses out of the canyon. There is no other way for a horse to leave the valley. A man who is strong and has Spirits guiding him can climb the sheer walls that surround the valley to leave. But not a horse."

Scrapper John looked at Sky and then at Dark Eagle Walking. "It don't sound easy, but that ain't stopped me before. Me an' Sky will ride outta that patch of rattlers like we was goin' for a Sunday walk, Grandfather. I ain't sure just how yet, but we'll do it."

Dark Eagle Walking looked very solemn. "There is only one more thing that I can tell you."

Sky and Scrapper John waited for Dark Eagle Walking to continue. The old Indian looked at the two boys closely, his dark eyes staring hard.

"The pass out of the valley where the fanged ones live," Dark Eagle Walking said solemnly, "it is called the Path of Death."

CHAPTER NINE

Scrapper John and Seeks The Far Sky rested in the Nez Perce camp for another day. Sky hadn't coughed once since his time in the sweat lodge. At first light on the third day, they finally set out. The two boys walked side by side through the forest, while Musket frisked about them, chasing after every stray scent. All three were glad to be on their way again.

After only two days of travel, they reached a broad plain covered with coarse buffalo grass. Many miles away, they saw a great wall of stone on the horizon, glinting in the sun. Great sheets of mica flashed and sparkled like the surface of a lake. Far to the north of the great wall, a great cloud of dust rose into the still air.

"What do you think that is?" Scrapper John asked. "Seems like it would take a powerful lot of animals or people to put that much dust in the air. My pa told me he seen a buffalo herd from far off one time when he was a boy. He said the cloud above them darkened the whole sky like a thunderstorm comin' up."

"My father told me of the buffalo herds, too," Seeks The Far Sky told Scrapper John. "He said that he saw one so big it took a day and half to go by. He saw white men shooting them from moving trains with rifles. The men on the trains left them to rot in the sun. They shot because they thought it was fun to kill buffalo. It made my father sick to talk of it."

"That sure ain't a buffalo herd out there, though," said Scrapper John. "My pa told me there ain't hardly enough woolies left to run in a herd. They're all killed now."

Seeks The Far Sky was silent as he thought for several moments. "It was white men with rifles that destroyed the buffalo herds. The Indians never killed like that."

The boys traveled in silence for an hour, each alone with his thoughts. Scrapper John was the first to break the silence. "Nothin' we can do about what's already happened to all them buffalo, Sky. The thing is, we can make sure we don't do nothin' that bad in our lives."

Sky smiled. "We can show by our friendship that white men and red men can be friends."

"What about red men an' half red an' half white boys?" Scrapper John asked, laughing.

"Them, too—and their half wolf, half dog creatures."

Just ahead, Musket froze, his nose pointing into a patch of low brush. Scrapper John held up his hand to quiet Sky. He unslung his bow from his back and notched an arrow. Sky watched curiously.

Scrapper John whistled quietly, and Musket lunged ahead into the bush, barking wildly. A half dozen fat quail thundered into the air, squawking up a storm. The mountain boy loosed an arrow that brought the largest one to earth.

"How did Musket know you wanted to take a quail for our meal?" Sky asked. "I didn't hear you—or see you—give him an order."

"His gut gave him an order." Scrapper John laughed. "Me an' Pa taught him to point out birds for us like that, an' now he does it when he's hungry. He figures if he wants to eat, so do we."

They stopped by a shallow pool of clear water to eat.

"Maybe we shouldn't start a fire," Sky said. "Something made all that dust earlier, and we could be calling trouble on ourselves."

"Trouble?" Scrapper John asked. "We ain't botherin' nobody. An' we sure ain't Indians on a battle party or a pack of soldiers huntin' down anybody. I say we cook up this quail right an' not worry 'bout our smoke."

Sky agreed, but only halfheartedly. He kept looking about as they gnawed on the cooked meat. Scrapper John noticed that his friend was uneasy.

"Look," he said, "what do you say we go over an' check out whatever is making all that dust?

You ain't gonna draw an easy breath until we do."

The two boys finished up their meal and carefully put out the fire. When they started walking again, they had to veer to the north to investigate the dust cloud. Scrapper John ordered Musket to stay close, adding, "An' quiet, boy. None of your yapping. We don't know who or what we're dealin' with, an' we don't need to give them no alarm."

The prairie rose gradually toward the roiling dust cloud. The ground was unbroken, and traveling fast was easy. The boys jogged through the ocean of buffalo grass, Musket trotting several yards ahead of them. Around them, snow-peaked mountains rose to the sky, and the only color other than cobalt blue sky was the long line of yellowish brown grit blowing up on the horizon. They slowed from a jog to a fast walk when the land began to angle sharply upward. Soon it turned into a wide, grassy slope. On the far side, where the dust cloud rose, the slope ended sharply at a ridge overlooking the grassy plains. It made a perfect lookout.

"We ain't gonna need ropes or jerky to do a little spyin'," Scrapper John told Sky. "An' we sure ain't plannin' on gettin' close enough to whatever's out there to need my bow or quiver. We can pick up our things after we've had a look-see." They halted and eased their packs of supplies off their backs.

Just before they came to the edge of the ridge, Scrapper John motioned Musket to sit. The two boys dropped to their bellies and crawled the few remaining feet. When they looked over the ridge, they were speechless.

On the plain below, from one end of the horizon to the other, stretched a long line of covered wagons pulled by teams of horses, mules, and steers. They heard the distant sounds of wooden axles squeaking, horses whinnying, the lolling sounds of the steers—and human voices as well. Men on horseback rode back and forth from wagon to wagon, many with dogs at their sides. The sun glinted on the barrels of the rifles and shotguns many of the men carried. Some boys riding bareback tended to a small herd of cattle, whistling at them and swinging their horses close to keep the herd moving alongside the wagon train. Every so often the sharp crack of a driver's whip carried like the sound of a shotgun.

"So many people—so many of them wagons. I never seen nothin' like this before in my whole life," Scrapper John said in awe.

"I have," Sky said.

"I wonder where they're goin'" Scrapper John said.

"It doesn't make much difference," Sky responded. "To the Blackfeet—and to all the tribes—the wagon trains mean only one thing: more fighting and more killing when they take land away from the Indian."

Both boys were uneasy about the stream of wagons on the plain below them, but both were fascinated by the sight as well. "Could be lots of them folks is real good people," Scrapper John said.

"Good people or not, they don't belong here," Sky said.

Although the sun was getting low, the mountain boy and the Indian continued their journey toward the wall of sparkling rock that hid the Valley of the Spotted Horses. They were able to reach it by dusk. The prairie halted abruptly at the mountain, as if the entire, towering rock face had been dropped suddenly from the clouds above. They camped in the shelter of a huge boulder nearby. The next morning they awakened early and after a quick breakfast of jerky got ready to climb the mountain.

"Sure is steep," Scrapper John said.

"We knew it would be. Feel how the wind grows stronger near the mountain? Just like your grandfather Dark Eagle Walking told us."

Musket whimpered and shoved his nose into Scrapper John's hand, asking to be scratched. "We got a little problem here," the mountain boy said.

"Yes. No dog in the world will be able to climb that wall with us—not even your Musket." Sky stepped over and ran his hand the length of the dog's back. "What will we do about him?"

Scrapper John had to swallow hard before he'd trust his voice. He hadn't been more than calling distance from his dog since the day Stone Pete had given him the pup, and that was six years ago.

"Ain't no big problem," he said. "Me an' my pa trained Musket to take care of himself when he needs to. He'll git along fine till we git back."

Scrapper John's voice cracked on the word "back." He swallowed again and snapped his fingers. Musket stared up into his face. "You hunt, boy, an' you stick around here. Me an' Sky, we'll be back for you, an' we'll be ridin' two of them spotted horses."

Musket whined in his throat. He understood what Scrapper John was saying, and he'd obey, but that didn't mean he had to like being left behind. When the boys started the climb, they were both careful not to look back. Musket watched them pick their way from ledge to ledge by finding handholds and pulling themselves up, higher and higher. The wolf-dog paced back and forth, whining mournfully as the two boys got smaller and smaller above him.

Scrapper John looked back once and saw Musket pacing and looking up at him and Sky. His heart went out to his dog, even though he knew it was impossible for Musket to follow. He realized that he himself was feeling a bit like Musket. He couldn't follow his father to where he'd gone either, but that didn't stop Scrapper John from missing Stone Pete and wishing he could be with him.

The wind became stronger and stronger as the boys climbed. They stopped picking their way up after an hour and sat on a small ledge, eating venison jerky. It seemed like the entire Great Plains were spread out before them, with snow-capped mountain ranges disappearing into the blue horizon.

Sky looked straight up to the top of the wall of

rock. "Looks like it gets a little harder from here on up. I can't see any good handholds or ledges between here and the top."

Scrapper John followed Sky's gaze. "Maybe we ought to tie ourselves together like Dark Eagle Walking told us."

He took his rope from his backpack, uncoiled it, and double wrapped it around his waist. Sky secured his rope to John's and wrapped the other end around his waist.

"I'll go first," Scrapper John insisted. He scrambled to his feet and began climbing before Sky could answer. Sky followed his friend with his eyes. When the mountain boy found an outcropping of rock to hold onto, Sky started up. He passed John and kept going until he found a secure rock to hold onto. Then it was John's turn again. It was a slow way to climb, but if one of them happened to slip and fall, the rope between the two boys would save him.

They climbed that way for the rest of the afternoon, moving past each other on the way up, sending clouds of pebbles and bits of stone tumbling down the rock face each time one of their moccasined feet slipped the slightest bit. It was hard, sweaty, and dangerous work, and they spoke very little.

Just as dusk arrived they reached the top of the wall of rock. Both boys were so exhausted they didn't even have the energy to celebrate. Instead, they just gave each other weary smiles.

They rested on a narrow plateau for a few moments. Then John got up and walked to the furthest edge to look over. Now he couldn't help whooping for joy.

"Sky!" he yelled. "We made it. It's the Valley of Spotted Horses."

Sky ran over and looked down. Although the light was almost gone, a small, twisting river reflected the colors of sunset. There were patches of trees scattered among stone outcroppings that were streaked with the same kind of mica that they'd seen on the wall they'd just climbed. Small ponds were scattered across the floor of the valley, partly surrounded by brush and young trees. The boys chewed jerky and looked out over the beautiful valley.

"The climb down to the floor shouldn't be too bad," Scrapper John said around a mouthful of the dried, salted venison. "Looks like there's plenty of water down there. Probably enough quail an' other birds to keep us eatin' good."

"There could be fish in the river and in the . . ."

The sound of far-off drumming cut Sky off in midsentence. The boys peered into the thickening darkness. For a split second, they saw something moving in the valley below. It was a snow white horse with spots on its rump, racing over the land as effortlessly as the wind. Scrapper John and Sky held their breaths and watched it disappear among some trees. Then the sound of hoofbeats faded with the last bit of light, and the valley was completely dark.

CHAPTER TEN

The next morning, the boys descended to the floor of the valley as soon as the sun came up. Tendrils of mist drifted lazily from the surface of the narrow river, and the trees were shrouded by wispy clouds. They roamed about, speaking softly to each other. Scrapper John laughed. "What're we talkin' so low for?"

"This is a magic valley," Sky said. "I can feel it."

"Maybe. But right now I'm more interested in grub than magic. Jerky ain't bad, but I need real food—like a few trout outta the river, there."

Sky couldn't help grinning at his friend. "There is one difference between the two of us, Scrapper John," he said. "I eat to live, but you live to eat. But I'm hungry, too. Maybe we should eat and set up a camp before we start looking for the spotted horses."

Scrapper John looked through his backpack for

his fishing line and hook. "I don't think we're gonna have to do much lookin', Sky. I figure them horses will come to us."

"Why? Why should they come to us? I don't understand."

Scrapper John waved his arm in a broad circle. "Look at all this—it's a perfect place for horses. They got no real enemies here, 'cept rattlers an' maybe a few mountain cats. Horses can smell snakes as fast as a dog can, and mountain cats ain't known for taking horses out of a herd. They'll run down an old horse or a young one if they git a chance, but it takes a real cold winter to git a cat to try hittin' a herd or anything close to a herd. See what I mean?"

Sky looked confused. "What does that have to do with the horses coming to us?"

"These spotted horses are supposed to be real smart. Smart means curious. Soon's they smell us they'll want to know who and what we are, an' they'll come to find out. They don't see us as enemies—jist different from what they're used to." Scrapper John grinned again. "You wait an' see if I ain't right, Sky. Meantime, let's go catch ourselves some breakfast."

The trout fishing wasn't much fun—it was too easy. In a matter of a very few minutes, Scrapper John caught four big ones. They built a quick fire and cooked the fish, seasoning the firm white meat with wild herbs Sky found growing near the river. After putting out the fire they decided to look for a campsite.

A half mile or so from where they'd come down

the rock face into the valley, Sky discovered a cave with a high, wide mouth facing the river. Its floor was dry and fairly level, and fresh air moved through it constantly.

"We sure ain't goin' to do no better'n this," Scrapper John said happily. "We're home for as long as it takes to grab a couple horses an' do some trainin'."

Sky was equally pleased. "I told you the valley was magic. It even gives us a fine home before we've been in it half a day. Let's gather up some grass to make our beds and . . ."

They both heard the low, distant drumming at the same time.

"Here they come," Scrapper John said. "I figured they'd be down to drink this mornin'. Let's go out there by the river an' just set still an' watch."

The boys found a wide, flat rock in full sunlight. They'd barely gotten comfortable when the herd of Appaloosas galloped out from beyond a rocky hill and raced for the river.

There were about a hundred horses all together, led by the white stallion they'd seen the night before. He was as tall as a thoroughbred, with long, finely formed legs. His coat was pure white except for the black spots on his rump. He moved with an arrogant grace, whinnying over his shoulder to the others when he caught the scent of the two boys.

Sky and Scrapper John had never seen a horse quite like this stallion. The herd skidded to a stop and held back as the stallion moved cautiously forward, nostrils wide, filtering the strange new smell. The horse stopped about twenty yards away and stared at the boys.

Six or eight of the horses in the herd began to trot to where the stallion stood, but he swung his head back at them, teeth bared, and whinnied loudly. They turned back quickly and joined the herd.

"Ain't no question who gives the orders an' who follows them," Scrapper John whispered. The stallion's ears pricked up at the sound.

"He's perfect," Sky said quietly. "Never have I seen a horse like him."

Scrapper John stood very slowly and waited for several moments before he took a step. The stallion snorted and danced nervously, watching the boy. Scrapper John took another step forward, then another. The stallion snorted again. This time it was almost a challenge. He reared, his front hooves striking at the empty air in front of him.

Scrapper John backed up. "I'm just lettin' him know he's the boss," he explained to Sky, talking in a normal tone of voice. "Talk to me. I want these horses to get used to our voices."

Sky spoke excitedly in a mix of English and the language of the Blackfeet. In both tongues, he used the words "perfect" and "beautiful" often. Scrapper John started moving ahead at a slow, even pace. When he was ten yards from the white horse, the stallion snorted and reared again. Then he spun around and dashed back to his herd, leading them downriver to drink elsewhere.

"They'll be back," Scrapper John promised. "You got your eye on a special one yet?"

"All of them are special. So many colors!"

"Some real fine young studs an' mares," Scrapper John agreed. "I'd sure like to git a rope on that white horse, but there ain't no way a man will ever ride him. He'd die before he'd give in to bein' trained."

Sky nodded. "He is the leader. We cannot take him. It would not be fair. But the others . . ." He stared after the herd. "When do we try to take our first horse?"

"Tomorrow. No sense in wastin' time. Let's spend today gettin' our camp set up—gatherin' firewood an' doin' some explorin'. I got to tie us a couple sets of hobbles, too."

"Hobbles? What are hobbles?"

"Nothin' fancy. Jist little loops of rope that go around the low part of a horse's front legs to keep him from runnin' off after we catch him."

That evening the boys ate trout again and turned in early. If things went well in the morning, they'd have their first spotted horse the very next day. In the cave, it was a long time before they slept. Bats flew in and out the cave entrance, darting to catch flying insects.

"One thing I didn't tell you 'bout tomorrow," Scrapper John said. "That white stud knows our scent now, and so do the others. They know we ain't enemies, but that don't mean they're gonna let us walk up an' say hello. If we're gonna catch one of them, we gotta make sure we're not seen— or smelled. That's all."

Sky was just dozing off when he snapped awake. "What do you mean that's all? Hiding isn't hard, but what about our scents?"

"That's the thing. 'Member all that nice, fresh manure the herd left behind today?"

Sky hesitated. "Yes."

"I hope you liked it, Sky. 'Cause tomorrow before first light you an' me is goin' to roll in it till we smell more like a heap of dung than people."

There was a long silence. "You're sure this will work?"

"I ain't dead sure of nothin', Sky." Scrapper John laughed. " 'Cept maybe that this cave is goin' to be kinda stuffy tomorrow night, no matter what."

Both boys were awake an hour before the sun shed any light into the valley. They found their way slowly through the early morning darkness to a spot where the herd had run the day before. Then they rolled around on the ground, laughing and flinging manure at each other.

By first light they were crouched in a natural pocket of rock. A few feet away, the banks of the river were covered with hoofprints. The two boys waited patiently, keeping perfectly still. It seemed like time had stopped. Seconds crawled by but somehow turned into minutes, and the minutes into an hour. After a while, their noses were used to the strong smell of the horse manure, and they barely noticed it. When the sound of drumming hooves reached them, Scrapper John shifted the coil of rope from his shoulder to his lap and made sure the loop at one end was wide open.

"You tell me which horse, Sky. If he's too far off, we'll wait him out. He'll be back tomorrow. I got to do it right an' quick. Pick him out an' point, an' I'll give it my best shot."

"We will take your horse first, Scrapper. It is only fair."

"Nope. Yours. Don't argue. This is your journey first, so you get the first one. Now, hush! They're gettin' close."

The stallion led the herd in, his nose suspiciously testing the air. The sun was bright enough for the colors of the Appaloosas to be seen clearly and sharply. When the stallion lowered his head to drink, the rest of the herd moved into the river behind him. They sucked at the cold water, jostling and splashing one another as they moved about.

"That one," Sky whispered with so much excitement that his voice trembled. "The roan next to the black. See him?"

Scrapper John nodded, the rope twitching in his hand. The moment the red horse with large white spots on his rump wandered close, John was ready to spring up and make his throw. Several times the roan started toward where the boys were hidden, but each time he veered away. Once he seemed to be staring directly at the two boys, and Scrapper John's palms began to sweat. When another young horse nudged the roan, he turned away.

Sky clenched his fists tightly to keep back his

impatience. The white stallion splashed out of the river and shook himself on the bank. Then he whinnied at his herd. Sky thought their chance to lasso the roan was lost for that day. The horses milled about, taking final drinks. Most of them followed the stallion to the riverbank. A black horse nipped at the roan's flank. The roan turned and reared, striking the black horse with his front hoof. The black ducked and floundered out of the river, running directly past Scrapper John and Sky.

The roan Appaloosa hadn't liked being nipped. He laid his ears back and ran after the black horse.

Scrapper John's throw was perfect. The loop snapped sharply and closed around the roan's neck.

The peaceful scene along the riverbank erupted into chaos. The stallion rushed at his charges, shoving them away from the river, using his teeth and hooves to get them moving. Scrapper John had counted on the stallion doing this. The white Appaloosa was too good a leader to stand and fight for one horse when the entire herd might be in danger. Instead, the stallion's concern was to get the rest of his horses away. Whinnying and snorting crazily, the herd of Appaloosas quickly disappeared into the trees, their hoofbeats thundering against the hard, dry earth.

Scrapper John and Sky were alone—with a crazy-mad roan Appaloosa horse on the end of a rope.

Sky grabbed at the rope just in front of Scrapper John's hands.

"Hold on with all you've got!" Scrapper John shouted.

The roan dragged the boys to the riverbed, whipping his head and squealing in high-pitched shrieks. Long strands of foaming spittle flew from his open mouth.

The boys' bare hands were scraped and burned by the rough rope, but both hung on tightly. The roan reared and struck, but Scrapper John and Sky threw their weight against him, pulling on the rope with all their strength to keep the horse's hooves on the ground.

The roan fought on even longer than Scrapper John had expected him to. When it seemed as if he were finally exhausted, the horse found even more strength and fought as if he'd just been roped. The boys worked the rope, their hands bleeding and their backs aching. At first they shouted words of encouragement to each other, but as the fight went on they found they needed to save their breath.

The battle became silent, except for the horse's high-pitched whinnying. Finally, the boys began to win. The horse was visibly tired and moving far less quickly. When the roan stopped to draw breath his head hung low. Scrapper John let Sky take the rope alone. Quickly, he whipped the hobbles from around his waist and rushed the Appaloosa.

Before the horse knew what had happened, his front legs were roped together with only a few

101

inches between them. Scrapper John leaped back as the roan reared back in anger. The horse came down off balance and slammed to the ground on his side. He wobbled slowly to his feet, squealing in the strange, shrill voice of a frightened horse. Again the roan tried to rear, and for the second time he crashed to the earth. Running was impossible. He jacked ahead several strides in a crow hop that did nothing but further enrage him.

Scrapper John stood back, rubbing the blood from his hands on the grass. Sky crouched, one foot a bit ahead of the other, and watched the horse's last struggles. His lips moved in a silent Blackfoot prayer. The roan shook his head from side to side, sucking in air, his sides heaving.

"Now, Sky!" Scrapper John yelled. "Now's the time! Show that horse who owns him!"

CHAPTER ELEVEN

Sky dashed toward the horse, the end of the rope still clutched in his hand. When the horse brought his head up, the Indian boy quickly spun the rope twice around the Appaloosa's throat. He grabbed a handful of mane and swung himself up onto the horse's sweating back.

The Appaloosa stood still for a long moment, his liquid brown eyes showing surprise and shock. Then he went berserk. He launched himself at the sky, throwing his body with his shoulders twisting like a snake in a frying pan, his teeth snapping together. Sky's right hand clutched the rope around the horse's neck, while he kept his left hand locked onto the mane. Putting all his strength into his legs to hold them tightly against the animal's sides, Seeks The Far Sky whooped a Blackfoot battle cry.

The Appaloosa hit the ground with all four hooves and spun crazily, his backbone contorting wildly. Sky whipped back and forth like a tree in a hurricane.

The Appaloosa sprang into the air again and swung his front end back toward his rear. Sky was thrown so hard, he took a handful of the horse's mane with him. He landed a dozen feet away.

Scrapper John quickly lassoed the roan and brought the horse's head down, while Sky slowly picked himself up, grimacing from some painful bruises. The Indian boy ran back and jumped on the wild horse.

It took almost two hours—and several hard spills—before Seeks The Far Sky had the roan Appaloosa ridden down. Finally, its muzzle dripping sweat and its sides heaving like leaky bellows, the animal stood quietly with Sky sitting proudly on his back.

Scrapper John howled in excitement. "You done it, Sky! You got yourself a spotted horse!"

Sky was so sore and exhausted he was shaking. But with manure sticking to his clothes and hair, his face covered with sweat and dirt, he still beamed with happiness.

"I will name him Blood Brother, because part of him is red like blood, and because it was my blood brother who helped me find him."

Later that day, Scrapper John cut armfuls of fresh grass and hauled them to a spot near the cave where Blood Brother would be kept. They kept the roan hobbled and would have to almost all the time until the boys felt he could be trusted not to bolt or to wander off. The hobbles allowed the roan to move around enough to graze for food, and there was good water nearby.

Sky spent the day rubbing the Appaloosa's coat with his hands and talking softly to gain the animal's trust. He fed handfuls of sweet grass to his new mount, murmuring in Blackfoot to him. By the end of the day, Blood was barely spooked when Sky approached and touched him.

The next morning the boys huddled in a clump of brush next to a drinking spot a mile or so from the one they'd used the day before. They'd rolled in manure again. Sky's muscles ached as if they were on fire, and his hands were raw and trembling. Scrapper John was a bit fresher than his friend, because he hadn't gone through two hours of bronc busting. Still, if all went well, he knew that by the end of the day he'd feel the exact same way.

While the boys waited by the water hole, the white stallion trotted up, his band farther behind him than the day before. He prodded the air with his nose for several minutes before whinnying to signal the herd. As the other horses charged into the water, the stallion drank a little but kept constant guard.

Scrapper John tensed as a black Appaloosa with white spots on his rump and around his eyes moved toward him. It was the same one that had nipped Blood Brother a day earlier. The horse plunged his face into the cool, clear water. The boy shifted his feet slightly, holding his breath. The horse was still too far away from the boys' hiding place for John to throw the lasso.

The stallion was beginning to shag his charges out of the water and back onto the riverbed. A young mare danced by the clump of brush that hid the boys, her hooves clicking on flat pieces of stone. The black horse eyed her and followed playfully, his tail held high as he shot out of the water. Scrapper John sprang up, whirled the rope, and threw.

The loop opened perfectly and settled gently down around the black's neck. It took the horse a second to realize what had happened. When he felt pressure on the rope, he began to fight.

The white stallion, snarling in fury at having been outsmarted again, whirled on his herd. He pushed the band away from the captured black horse, punishing them with his teeth when they didn't move fast enough and glaring back over his shoulder. His eyes met Scrapper John's for a split second, and the boy could sense the stallion's hatred.

"We ain't gonna bother your herd no more," he shouted. "An' we'll take real good care of the two horses we grabbed!" The stallion whinnied angrily, turned, and galloped after his herd without a second look back.

The black Appaloosa was in a frenzy, fighting the rope with all his strength. Scrapper John and Seeks The Far Sky dug their heels into the soft ground near the river. This horse was stronger than the roan and trickier, too. He used the length of the rope to his own advantage, whipping his body and flinging the boys back and forth. He charged them twice, striking at them with his teeth clattering madly as he lunged.

Scrapper John decided the horse was so wild that it was time for drastic measures. He hated to hit any animal, but a charging thousand-pound stallion was as dangerous as a runaway steam locomotive. The third time the black Appaloosa charged, he dropped his right hand from the rope, positioned his legs, and threw all his weight into a punch. He slammed his fist into the black horse's soft, sensitive nostrils.

The Appaloosa drew to an abrupt halt. He snorted and shook his head in pain, but he didn't charge the boys again. Even so, it took two more hours with both boys fighting from the other end of the rope before the black horse grew tired and bowed its head in defeat.

Without using the hobbles, Scrapper John raced to him, wrapped the rope twice around his neck, and swung onto his back.

The Appaloosa screeched in anger and started to scramble around in tight circles, slinging mud and chasing his tail while he bucked up and down. Scrapper John hung on, hollering and whooping, thrilled at the speed and power of his new mount. His head whiplashed back and forth wildly. He slammed his nose into the horse's neck. Blood cascaded down his face and onto his manure-stained jacket.

It was another two full hours before the black Appaloosa stood still, the battle over. Scrapper John had been thrown twice, once partially into the river. He was coated with mud and slime, and his face was bloody. He nodded to Sky to slip the hobbles on. When the Indian boy was finished, he stepped back, smiling at his friend.

"Now we both have spotted horses from this valley," he said. "The real training can begin."

Scrapper John rubbed the Appaloosa's grimy, sweaty neck. "Yep," he managed to croak from his dry throat. "And then all we gotta do is get outta this here valley!"

CHAPTER TWELVE

For the next two weeks, Scrapper John and Sky were with their new horses constantly. They fed them by hand and petted them all the time, talking out loud to the horses. Gradually, they were able to form a bond of trust with the animals that would last a lifetime.

Sky showed Scrapper John how to make hackamores, bridles that put pressure on sensitive points along the horse's muzzle. John cut lengths of rope for reins. With hackamores and reins, they would be able to control the horses while they were riding, steering them in the right direction and setting their speed.

Each horse had a distinctive personality. Scrapper John's black stallion proved to have blinding speed, but Sky's red horse had longer endurance. Scrapper John's biggest problem was deciding on a name for his horse. One afternoon, he and Sky were feeding Blood Brother and the spotted black

Appaloosa handfuls of grass. Both boys had been throwing suggestions into the air.

"There are some good names there, Sky," Scrapper John said. "But there aren't none of 'em that seem right somehow."

"The name will come to you when it is time," Seeks The Far Sky told his friend. "And you will be sure it is the right one."

Ten days later, Scrapper John and Sky set off on horseback toward the only escape route from the Valley of the Spotted Horses. The two Appaloosas were frisky in the early morning coolness. Both were well broken and responded to orders from their riders, but they were still green—they couldn't really be counted on to behave correctly in all situations. That would come only with time and with many, many months of riding.

Sitting astride their mounts, the two boys picked their way down the length of the beautiful valley, stopping often to let their horses drink and eat sweet buffalo grass.

"This ain't gonna be easy, Sky," Scrapper John said before they reached the pass that led out of the valley. "These boys is doin' real good, but snakes spook even the best horses."

Sky patted his horse's neck affectionately. "We have captured and trained two of the finest horses in the world. Now we'll find a way out."

Scrapper John smiled. "You got a point there. Nothin's stopped us yet. Maybe nothin' never will. Not even the Path of Death that Dark Eagle Walking told us about."

They came upon the end of the valley suddenly.

A narrow pass perhaps a hundred feet wide led between two sheer walls of rock. Veins of mica glittered in the stone. The ground was littered with hundreds of flat gray rocks.

The sun baked down on the dry land, and the air was as hot as an oven. Sky sniffed, aware of a strange scent.

"The smell of vipers," he said solemnly. "I have smelled it before."

"I smell it, too," said Scrapper John.

The scent reached the Appaloosas, and their instincts caused them to dance nervously. The boys held their horses steady and gazed out into the narrow pass. They had no way of knowing how far it was to the other side. It looked as if the flat, sun-baked rocks were littered with twigs and broken tree branches.

"I wonder where all them sticks an' such came from," Scrapper John mused. "Ain't no trees or brush in that pass—nothin' but stone."

"Look more closely," Sky said. "Sticks don't move. Rattlers do."

Scrapper John stared ahead and gulped. The warm rocks were covered with the thick bodies of fat rattlesnakes basking in the warm sun. The boys got down from their mounts and hobbled them, leaving them to graze well away from the dangerous pass.

The two boys approached on foot. As they neared the pass, they heard the low steady buzz of rattlers.

"Look," Scrapper John told Sky. He pointed toward a pile of bones bleaching in the sun.

There was a large rib cage, all that remained of an unlucky horse.

Sky nodded, chewing his lower lip. Other skeletons littered the pass, some that looked like coyotes, others larger.

"Mountain cat over there," Scrapper John said, pointing again.

"And look there—past the tall rock in the middle," Sky said, gulping. The skeleton there was unmistakably human. It was picked clean of flesh and partly covered in tattered bits of cloth. As the boys stared, a long, fat rattlesnake slid out of an empty eye socket in the skull.

"Poor guy was probably jist tryin' to git outta here with a good horse," Scrapper John said.

"Now we know the truth of Dark Eagle Walking's words," said Sky. "This way surely has been the Path of Death for many."

That night the boys sat at their camp fire. They talked very little. An air of frustration had settled over them.

"There's gotta be a way to get out of here, dang it." Scrapper John snorted. "We ain't gonna be beat by no bunch of snakes."

"There is a way," Sky assured him. "Others have done it. All we have to do is find that way. We will."

"Yeah, but when? We could be old men before we leave this valley."

For the next two days, Scrapper John and Seeks The Far Sky explored the pass and the area around it. It became clear that there was no other way out of the valley on horseback, except through the rattlesnake-filled pass. They could climb the walls without too much difficulty, but a horse couldn't make it.

"Maybe a fire in the pass would git enough of the snakes out of the way for us to make a run for it," Scrapper John suggested at the camp fire one night.

"It might. But what would we burn, Scrapper? There's no wood or grass in the pass. And it would take us many moons to carry enough in to make it work. We don't even know how long the pass is."

Scrapper John sighed. "You're right." He stood and slapped at a mosquito with more force than was needed. "This is drivin' me crazy," he growled. "There's got to be a way, Sky, but how do we find it?"

"I . . . I'm not sure. We will. You have to believe that. A sign will come to us. All we can do is wait."

"I'm plain sick of waitin', Sky!"

"Try some sleep," Sky suggested quietly. "You won't find an answer punching mosquitos, my friend. Let the Spirits work. Think of your father. What would he do?"

"I don't know, and he sure ain't here to tell me," Scrapper John answered hotly.

"He is always with you," Sky answered softly.

"Yeah," Scrapper John said after a moment. "I know you're right about my pa. I been thinkin' 'bout him a lot. He'd know a way to git outta this valley with our horses. He knew lots of things that I didn't have time to learn. I sure miss him

113

a whole lot—an' I'm right sorry for snappin' at you like I done, Sky. I guess I'll turn in. Maybe things will look better in the mornin'."

Scrapper John twisted and turned on his bed of grass for a long time before sleep came to him. His mind swirled with images of rattlers and horses, the mountain pass, and the white bones bleaching on the sun-baked ground. Finally, he slept and fell into a deep dream. He was walking along the bank of a muddy river that ran strong after a heavy rain. A rotting log bobbed in the current, and on top of it was a swarm of snakes, hissing and rattling as they writhed together like tangled hair.

Scrapper John sat bolt upright and yelled, "I got it, Sky! I got the way out!"

Quickly, he explained his dream to his friend.

"All we need is a powerful rainstorm to sweep them snakes outta our way. Then we ride for all we're worth. We can do it! All we need is the rain!"

For three days, Scrapper John and Sky scanned the sky, hoping for some sign of a storm.

"It ain't rained since we've been in the valley," Scrapper John said. "Maybe it never rains here."

"It rains everywhere, Scrapper," Sky said. He led Scrapper John to the rocky cliffs on one side of the entrance to the Path of Death and pointed to some faint lines in the stone.

"Sometimes the river in the valley floods over its banks and flows through the pass. When it does, it leaves these lines in the rock. Perhaps the river grows bigger when the mountain snows melt in the spring. Or maybe when it rains very hard in the summer. I cannot say, but we must hope for rain."

Two more days dawned warm and clear. The weather was depressingly, disappointingly, perfect. The two friends practiced racing their horses, making them sprint as fast as they could for short distances.

At the camp fire that night, Scrapper John gnawed on a quail drumstick. "We gotta make a run for it, Sky," he said. "These two horses are ready as they're ever gonna be. And so are we."

"Not without the rain we need. It would be sure death. But I have an idea, Scrapper. It may not make sense to you, but it does to me and to my people. We can call a storm on us. There are dances and songs that the Blackfeet use to call the Spirits of Wind and Rain. I know some of these dances."

Scrapper John laughed. "This ain't no time to joke, Sky."

When the Indian turned away, the mountain boy looked closely at his friend.

"You mean it, don't you? You really think a rain dance can work?"

Sky stood. "I do. Come. If you like, I will teach you."

The boys danced and sang for hours until they dropped from exhaustion. Sky's voice was raspy, and his throat burned. Scrapper John's was little better. Their fire had burned itself to embers and gone out. The sky above them was as clear as a mountain pool, and the stars were so bright they looked close enough to touch. Their hopeful eyes scanned the heavens from one side to the other. It was a perfect summer night.

"We done the best we could," Scrapper John consoled Sky.

The Indian boy shook his head sadly. "Perhaps if I had paid more attention to the dances when I saw the medicine man do them, maybe . . ." His words trailed away to silence.

"Hey, come on," Scrapper John said, giving him a friendly punch in the shoulder. "That's like sayin' if a bear had wings, he could fly. It don't make no sense. You can't blame yourself."

But in his heart, Scrapper John was as sad as Sky. The rain dance had failed.

The boys dropped off to sleep without much more conversation. A few yards away, the black Appaloosa and Blood grazed at the sweet buffalo grass. A light breeze tugged at their manes and tails as they ate.

While he slept, Scrapper John brushed at his face and turned to roll over on his other side. He brushed his face again, sighing. Then, as if an inner voice awakened him, he opened his eyes. At that moment, a big, fat drop of rain splashed against his nose.

He jumped to his feet shrieking, "Sky! It's raining! It's raining!"

The Blackfoot boy opened his eyes and looked skyward. The stars had disappeared under a blanket of black clouds. In a second he was up, whooping and laughing with his friend. Thunder rumbled overhead, and tongues of lightning flashed. The raindrops grew bigger and came faster.

The two boys gathered up their backpacks and raced to their horses. The rain was pounding down by the time the horses were ready, collecting in puddles on the ground. Already the river had grown fatter. Strong winds pushed the rain in sheets up the narrow pass, and runoff down the sheer rock walls collected in pools on the ground.

Scrapper John eased his horse into the entrance to the pass. The rain was pelting him and his horse. Rattlesnakes hissed and writhed across the wet ground, searching for dry shelter under rocks.

"We need more water," Scrapper shouted over the noise of the thunder and rain. "If only . . ."

Then the boys heard something roar behind them.

"Flash flood!" Scrapper John yelled.

"We must find higher ground, my friend!" Seeks The Far Sky shouted at him.

They nudged their horses with their heels, and the two Appaloosas responded as they had been trained. They galloped to the top of a hill on one side of the canyon. A wall of brown water from the overflowing river swept toward the pass. Thunder crashed, and the rains and wind lashed them. The water rushed into the pass, rolling large rocks out of its path, scattering bones, pitching snakes in all directions, and sweeping them away.

The horses were wide-eyed and snorting. The

boys held them on tight reins, watching and waiting for the perfect moment. The thunder sounded farther away, and soon the rain began to thin. The level of the water dropped quickly. Soon it was only a foot deep. It swirled, muddy and swift through the Path of Death.

Scrapper John reached his hand out to his friend. Seeks The Far Sky took it, and they gripped each other's hand tightly.

"You 'bout ready, Sky?" Scrapper John asked.

The Indian nodded.

They galloped at full speed down the hill, whooping and shouting, and blasted into the entrance of the Path of Death. The rushing water swirled around the horses' legs, while the animals' eyes drilled into the darkness in front of them. Flashes of lightning revealed snakes that had found safety on flat boulders. The vipers lashed out, baring their deadly white fangs at the horses and their riders. The thunder boomed overhead and echoed back and forth between the walls of the pass like heavy drums.

The horses galloped through the racing water, propelled by terror, sometimes slipping and catching their balance. A rattler struck at Scrapper's horse and barely missed. The Appaloosa whinnied in terror.

The boys held on tightly as their mounts took them further and further down the pass. They shrieked as they rode, encouraging the horses and yelling at them to run faster. The thunder grew louder again, exploding next to their heads and reverberating up and down the walls of the narrow canyon. Lightning flashed almost constantly. With each bolt, Scrapper John's horse ran faster. Snakes with glowing black eyes and bloodred tongues churned along in the waters of the flood.

Scrapper John saw a rattler flung against his horse's flank by the waves. The snake fell back into the water before it could bite. John shouted above the noise of the storm and banged his heels against the horse's sides to urge him on faster.

A moment later, the pass curved between two cliffs and ended. In the darkness beyond, rocky slopes led down to a thick forest and plains of buffalo grass far below. Scrapper John and Sky bolted through at a full gallop.

Soaking wet and panting from the hard ride, the two boys raced on for a hundred yards and veered off. The rushing water swept into a gully that fed it down the mountainside. They drew rein fifty yards away.

"We done it!" Scrapper John yelled. "We done it, Sky!"

Sky grabbed his friend's shoulder, a smile splitting his face. "Of course we did! Friends like us can do anything!"

"Did you see this ol' horse go for it?" John exclaimed. "He went fast as lightning!" The mountain boy's face lit up. "That's it, Sky! That's his name—Black Lightning."

Seeks The Far Sky smiled and nodded. "Blood Brother and Black Lightning. We have named our horses well."

Scrapper John leaned forward in his saddle and

stroked Black Lightning's sleek, muscular neck. He knew that his father would have been proud to see Black Lightning tied in front of their cabin. Stone Pete had been a fine rider and an excellent judge of horses, and he'd taught Scrapper John just about everything he knew. The boy settled into the easy rhythm of Black Lightning's trot, his mind drifting back to the day his father fought the one-eyed grizzly. A lump rose in his throat. He missed Stone Pete. The mountain man had been more than just a father to Scrapper John. He'd been the boy's best friend.

Scrapper John remembered when he'd set his horse free in keeping with the old Indian custom. He knew his father would have approved. And with Sky riding next to him, Scrapper John realized that the Indian boy had taken away some of the hurt he'd felt after his father's death. No one would ever replace Stone Pete in Scrapper John's mind or heart, but Sky had shown him that good friends could help ease the pain that was part of life. The mountain boy closed his eyes for a moment, missing Stone Pete. When he opened them the lump was still in his throat, but he grinned at Sky and patted Black Lightning's neck again.

The two boys rode through the rain, putting another mile between themselves and the flash flood and the snakes. When they stopped at the edge of the forest, the thunder was moving away. Even the rain let up. The clouds broke, allowing starlight through. They listened to the sounds of the storm grow fainter for several minutes.

Scrapper John and Seeks The Far Sky dismounted and looked their horses over to make sure everything was all right. They patted the Appaloosas' muzzles. Scrapper John was just about to speak when the boys heard an animal crashing through the brush in the nearby forest. Instantly, both of them were alert. Sky pulled his knife from his sheath, and Scrapper John reached for his bow.

Then, in the darkness, the animal started barking frantically.

"Musket!" the boys shouted together.

A moment later, the wolf-dog burst from the trees, ran through the buffalo grass, and threw himself at Scrapper John with such eagerness he knocked the boy over. Between his laughter and Musket's tongue licking his face, the mountain boy could barely breathe.

"He found his way around the mountain all by himself," Scrapper John said between laughs. When Musket had calmed down a few minutes later, Scrapper John knelt by his wolf-dog, stroking his fur. Finally, Sky spoke.

"I was given four seasons to bring home a spotted horse from the valley. We have used only a small part of that."

"We can do a lot in the months you have left, Sky," Scrapper John said. "I want you to come back to my cabin with me."

"I would like to go with my friend," the Blackfoot boy said, nodding.

Scrapper John and Seeks The Far Sky grinned

at each other. They climbed onto Black Lightning and Blood Brother and, with Musket racing after them, galloped away from the Valley of the Spotted Horses.

Look for
SHOWDOWN AT BURNT ROCK
The next exciting adventure of
Scrapper John and his Blackfoot friend Sky

Stories of Adventure From
THEODORE TAYLOR
Bestselling Author of
THE CAY

TEETONCEY
71024-2/$3.50 US/$4.25 Can

Ben O'Neal searched the darkened shore for survivors from the ship wrecked by the angry surf. He spotted the body on the sand—a girl of about ten or eleven; almost his own age—half drowned, more dead than alive. The tiny stranger he named Teetoncey would change everything about the way Ben felt about himself.

TEETONCEY AND BEN O'NEAL
71025-0/$3.50 US/$4.25 Can

Teetoncey, the little girl Ben O'Neal rescued from the sea after the shipwreck of the *Malta Empress*, had not spoken a word in the month she had lived with Ben and his mother. But then the silence ends and Teetoncey reveals a secret about herself and the *Malta Empress* that will change all their lives forever.

THE ODYSSEY OF BEN O'NEAL
71026-9/$3.50 US/$4.25 Can

At thirteen, Ben O'Neal is about to begin his lifelong dream—to go to sea. But before Ben sails, he receives an urgent message from Teetoncey, saying she's in trouble. And somehow Ben knows that means trouble for him.